Deep in the remote, windswept wastes of Siberia, ingeniously hidden and already operational, lies a deadly new weapons system installed by the Soviets—far more advanced than its most sophisticated Western counterpart.

Unknown to the Kremlin, to the President, or to the public-at-large, the Pentagon has discovered Russia's secret and made its decision. Captain d'Alembert of the *Adresteia* has been given his orders: Find and destroy it!

Forced to choose between defiance and a command that will bring the world to the brink of irrevocable chaos, d'Alembert, too, must take a calculated risk . . . aware that the odds are stacked against him—and in favor of nuclear doom!

POSEIDON'S
SHADOW

A. P. Kobryn

A DELL BOOK

Published by
Dell Publishing Co., Inc.
1 Dag Hammarskjold Plaza
New York, New York 10017

Dell ® TM 681510, Dell Publishing Co., Inc.

ISBN: 0-440-16899-6

Reprinted by arrangement with Rawson, Wade Associates,
Publishers, Inc.

Printed in the United States of America

First Dell printing—December 1980

Such was their burial of Hektor,
breaker of horses.

CHAPTER 1

The United States' Ballistic Missile Submarine SSBN *Adresteia* was to sail at midnight.

The crew on the foredeck circled the lines swiftly into their lockers, securing them for the duration of the patrol. They worked in silence.

"Singled forward, sir."

"Secure all hatches forward."

"Aye, aye, sir."

The night was dark. Snow fell.

The crew chief called to the conning tower.

"Singled forward, Mr. Fox."

The executive officer looked into the darkness forward. The curved hull was slippery with the falling snow. He looked quickly aft.

"Singled aft, Mr. Fox."

The captain stood silent to Fox's left.

"Cast off aft, forward. Deck crew below."

The men carefully made their way to the doors at either side of the sail's base as *Adresteia* backed slowly from her slip and into the channel.

The captain noted the time at which they slipped free of their berth: 0001.

It was the twenty-first of December.

* * *

Looking Glass swept her wings high over Nebraska. Silent to the morning fields below, her contrails graced her course.

There was always an aircraft assigned as an emergency national command center if all else were to fail. Always airborne, one replacing another in constant turn, always a very high-ranking general in command, always identified as Looking Glass.

Within the windowless circumference of the flight's cabin some eighty men were at their accustomed posts, numbering the hours of their shift in numberless cups of coffee. In four hours' time another plane—their twin—would be airborne, would be Looking Glass, and their great gray 747 would begin the long descent to Omaha.

Till that time they were Looking Glass.

Till that time the man in the command section, General Malcolm N. Mann, USAF, Chairman of the Joint Chiefs of Staff, was Looking Glass.

Was command.

The submarine, its mass low in the water, moved in deathly silence. She came steadily about, clearing the waters of Puget Sound and entering the Strait of Juan de Fuca.

"I'll take the con, Charles."

"Aye, aye, sir."

"Get yourself a cup of coffee. Then take a turn through the boat."

"Right, Skipper."

Fox dropped quickly down the sail ladder and on through the hatch into the pressure hull. The control room was lit, while they ran on the surface, in red.

Stewart, *Adresteia*'s engineering officer, stood over the helmsmen.

"All well, Mr. Stewart?"

"Yes, Mr. Fox. All's well."

"Good."

Fox descended another level, to the officers' wardroom. The small space was empty, lit with the same red light as the control room. He drapped his jacket over the back of a chair, drew himself a mug of black coffee.

He sipped quietly at the coffee, which tasted strangely of the sea. The cup steamed angrily in the light.

Adresteia neared the Pacific. Prepared to dive.

General Mann was alone in the small conference room aboard Looking Glass, waiting.

The display screens that could present analyses of situations in any part of the world, syntheses of countless forms of information, were blank. The room lights were dimmed.

Mann thought, knowing *Adresteia* neared the Pacific, neared the time to submerge. His sixty-year-old face was shadowed as he thought—of the time. No longer thinking. Merely waiting. For the time.

His face was determined. It looked steadily ahead. Waiting.

The captain was alone atop the ship's tall sail, though the lookouts flanked him.

Adresteia made her way darkly to the sea. Running softly surfaced, she drew the waters of the strait slowly over her bow.

He drew at his pipe for warmth. Snowflakes patterned themselves against the glow, consumed.

The open sea sounded of night. He knew they were near. One hour free of the strait and *Adresteia* might sound the ocean.

It was nearly time.

Mann rose suddenly from his chair, crossed the small room, turned on the lights full bright. No longer a young man, he was still capable of decisive movement.

Still, he made it his practice, in matters of importance, to consider carefully before committing himself. He did not need to look at the chronometer to know the time. He stood, quite still, quite calm, recalling the relevant facts to mind, placing them precisely in their proper sequence.

The decision stood.

He summoned his aide, sat down to write out the few necessary words. The aide entered.

"Send this to *Adresteia*. Encrypted. Over Nav-Synch. Immediately."

The aide made no sound, acknowledging the order, closing the door behind himself.

Mann was alone again. The thing was done now, irrevocable. They were committed. He considered the empty display screens that formed the essential focus of the conference room, the complement of its primary focus—the oval table where decisions were to be made. He listened, momentarily, to the roar of the stratosphere as Looking Glass forced a constant passage.

He should find some deep significance in the moment, in the subliminal roar of the wind, he thought. But he found none.

The word would find its way swiftly to *Adresteia* and to d'Alembert, who awaited it, knowing.

Adresteia knew deep water beneath her keel. They had entered the Pacific Ocean, leaving the Olympic Peninsula behind them.

Fox climbed quickly to the top of the conning tower, where d'Alembert still had the con. The executive officer was jacketless, and he braced himself against the cold night wind as he emerged from the shelter of the sail to stand beside his captain. The depth of the overcast, the night, had shallowed somewhat. The captain was a tall, dark shape against the still descending snow.

"Message 'for your eyes only,' Skipper."

D'Alembert looked directly ahead.

"Read it."

Fox unfolded the piece of paper with numbing fingers.

" 'Vengeance is mine; I . . .' "

D'Alembert completed the sentence for him.

" '—will repay, saith the Lord.' "

D'Alembert said nothing for a time, gave no sign. He drew at his pipe. Fox waited in the cold and darkness beside his captain.

"Take the control room, Charles."

"Right."

"Prepare to dive."

"Aye, aye, Captain."

"I'll take her now, Bob."

"Very well, Mr. Fox."

Fox took the position that the engineering officer left, noted the readings.

"Gentlemen, prepare to dive."

Two minutes later the executive officer's voice reported through the sail's speaker.

"Prepared to dive on your order, Captain."

"Very well, Mr. Fox."

D'Alembert ordered the lookouts below. He rapped his pipe against the sail cowling, returned it to its pouch, the pouch to his jacket pocket. Slowly he turned full circle, scanning for an invisible horizon.

A snowflake brushed his lips.

"Ahead two-thirds."

"Ahead two-thirds."

Adresteia began to accelerate, the water sliding faster over the bow, pressing hard against the base of the sail. It streamed the full length of the hull now, covering even the long section aft of the conning tower where *Adresteia*'s missiles were housed. Only the sail stood free of the water, snow lightening the dark surface of the diving planes.

D'Alembert spoke, softly, to himself.

"Mine, indeed."

The ship continued to accelerate.

He called below.

"Take her down, Mr. Fox."

CHAPTER 2

D'Alembert dogged the pressure hatch shut as he dropped into the submarine's control room.

"Sail and pressure hull hatches secure, Mr. Fox."

"Very well, Captain. Diving officer?"

"Straight board, Mr. Fox."

"Depth, Skipper?"

"Fifty meters, Mr. Fox."

"Take her to five zero meters, Warren."

"Aye, aye, sir, five zero meters."

Adresteia grew steadier as she descended, no longer rolling with the waves. In her element.

"Five zero meters, sir."

D'Alembert turned to the engineering officer. "Mr. Stewart, how do you read the boat?"

"Nominal, Captain."

"Very well, Mr. Stewart. Mr. Fox, take her to four hundred meters proximate, present course, standard speed."

"Aye, aye, Skipper."

D'Alembert surveyed the control room.

"Then give the con to Mr. Stewart and report directly to my cabin."

Fox's voice betrayed no emotion.

"Aye, aye, Captain."

The executive officer rapped lightly on the captain's door.

"Come in, Charles."

Fox entered, his more than professional curiosity more than professionally masked. D'Alembert noted this, approved.

"Take a seat."

Fox sat on the captain's bunk, the only seat available to him in the small room. He looked openly, expectantly, toward d'Alembert, who now pushed his chair back from the desk at which he had been writing, faced him.

D'Alembert, in his turn, considered Fox openly, testing the man in his mind, judging him one final time. Then he nodded—in part to himself, in part to Fox—effectively ending the silence. He offered Fox a slim file of papers.

"Read it."

He waited.

Fox's first reaction to the material, the greater part of which was in raw numerical form, was one of sheer incredulity. He refused, as yet, to permit the full development of his second reaction, but read the papers through without looking up. Finally, he did look up.

D'Alembert had not lifted his eyes from Fox for an instant.

"Well?" he asked him.

"Well, what, Captain? What the hell is this supposed to mean?"

He tossed the papers back on the captain's desk.

"Exactly what it implies. We are to target three missiles on those three targets."

"The hell we are. Not as long as it takes my key among others to do it, we're not."

When d'Alembert spoke again, he spoke softly.

"I think, Charles, if it comes to it, we will launch on the necessary three targets. I think, too, that I will have your key. And the engineering officer's. And the weapons officer's."

Fox waited a moment before he spoke.

"Alex, what kind of madness is this?"

"Not mine, Charles. Not mine. I think I'd better explain."

"Yes, Captain. I think you'd better begin to explain."

Adresteia, invisible in the ocean in which she moved, sailed on into the Pacific. Ever deeper in the ocean, ever farther from the coast and home. Her executive officer began to learn of their situation, the particular form of their peril—a form which had been fashioned for them some time earlier.

It had begun routinely enough. Their Keyhole designations were numbers 317701, 317789, and 317811. Soviet antisatellite installations—ASATs in acronym—of recent construction. Each phase of construction was carefully scrutinized by the orbiting satellites. The Keyhole classifications were confirmed solid. The missiles were direct-to-orbit hot-metal interceptors targeted on Chinese communications and reconnaissance satellites. They presented no credible threat to the more sophisticated American satellites but were quite capable of shattering the relatively fragile Chinese military communications net. The Chinese were duly informed of much of the American intelligence and assured that any use of the ASATs would be considered an extremely serious act indeed. To what extent this assured Chinese confidence in their threatened command net is uncertain.

What is certain is that, six months later, there was an anomaly in the American analysis. A minor Soviet defector made a cryptic remark in debriefing which seemed to suggest that things were not what they seemed at the 317701 site. The man would say nothing further.

CIA was more than sufficiently aware that this might be bait of some sort, and fully a month was spent attempting to clarify the matter. At that point General Mann, as Chairman of the Joint Chiefs, was approached. CIA had concluded that this might, indeed, be a lure to force a U-2 type incident, but that satellite reconnaissance would no longer suffice. There was the perception of an urgent need to know more about those three sites. CIA's recommendation was that Stealth be employed.

Mann's decision was risky, Stealth's technical superiority notwithstanding. It was never routine to dispatch an intruder aircraft into Soviet airspace.

As per previous understandings, Mann did not consult with President Elliott. The decision was to be his alone. The responsibility would be his alone. If it were to go awry, presidential deniability would be assured.

Twenty-four hours later, Stealth was in position for the mission deep into Siberia.

* * *

Stealth, or, more precisely, Stealth F, sixth variant of the original project, was painted in shades of deepest gray, an eerily streamlined deltoid aircraft of almost alien aspect. It was most often referred to as "Blackbird'" though the nickname was first applied to a distant predecessor. Officially, neither nickname nor aircraft existed.

It had landed in Alaska in nightfall, taxiing swiftly down a darkened taxiway, hidden behind the glare of its lights. It rolled smartly into a darkened hangar. The doors closed.

A few hours later, a small helicopter hovered before the same hangar. The lights were extinguished, the hangar doors opened. Guided only by its landing lights, the helicopter flew cautiously into the hangar, the doors rolling quickly closed behind it as it extended its landing gear and settled tentatively to the floor.

The lights came on. A young man stepped out, considered the strange shape of the Stealth F that was to bear him, the dark mass of its hybrid form. Each aspect of the airplane's configuration, he knew, showed the most subtle of curvatures. Every component of airframe and power plant had been selected for minimum electronic signature.

Impressive as was the form of the black beast, the core of the aircraft was its electronics payload. Sophisticated enough to deceive the most sophisticated of sensors. Sophisticated enough, they hoped, to probe 317701 without detection. Stealth was not, literally, invisible, but it was, electronically, very nearly so. No one knew this better than Kenneth Jamison, NSA's ranking systems expert, young man though he was. Many of the systems were of his design.

Jamison was introduced to the pilot, a resolutely cheerful sort, as they suited up. Jamison, preoccupied, said very little. It was his job to get the information they needed, it was the pilot's job to take him where he needed to be taken. It was better for both that that was the beginning and the end of the matter.

The pilot, Colonel Young, had his own distinct set of preoccupations. This would be the deepest penetration of Soviet airspace ever attempted. It was his job to get them there and get them back. A singularity.

Airborne. Well within Soviet airspace. Nearing their objective.

Jamison had only two tiny windows in the mass of titanium that covered him. Strapped into the black hole of a cockpit behind the pilot, wearing a full pressure suit, secured in place by straps, wires, hoses, sitting in an armed ejection system, unable even to see the pilot in front of him, Jamison was nothing if not physically helpless, a prisoner of the mission. Yet the control, the direction, of that mission was his. He ignored the windows, which offered only a perspective on darkness, concentrated on the digital processors that yielded a steady stream of light.

"Colonel, give me two degrees left of present heading, please."

"Roger."

"Good."

Stealth was built for speed. The maneuverability of the dogfighter was not hers. She was meant to be an invisible intruder, surpassingly swift. Yet her maximum speed was next to useless, for it would compromise her mission in a hostile environment, increase her electronic presence. If they were detected, they had the speed to escape. But if they were detected, they had failed.

"Colonel, please program your VNAV for mission profile."

"Already done, sir."

"Nice, Colonel. Call me 'Ken.' All my friends—and most of my enemies—do. Begin the run on my mark, if you would. . . ."

"Ready."

"Now."

Neither man saw the site as they made their great probing sweep. Young had the best view, but there was nothing below but night. Jamison had no view, but knew everything that could be immediately known as site 317701's sentry radars swept, failed to detect them.

Jamison knew, too, within seconds of summarized data, that there was something very anomalous indeed about this site.

The pass was completed.

"Colonel, I need another pass—seventy-three degrees east of the initial run."

"Ken, do you really think . . . ?"

"—Yes."

"Give me the numbers."

Jamison had to rely on the computerized summaries of the masses of information being gathered on every available wavelength. The summaries suggested that the second pass gave him most of what he needed to know—and made it abundantly clear that he needed to know more. Another mission could not be risked. They must leave no room for uncertainty.

"Colonel, give me a tight orbit at sixty thousand."

There was a very long two-second pause from the forward cockpit.

"You got it."

They descended, began a great circling sweep of the site. Young began to sweat. Jamison watched the displays as Stealth's electronic countermeasures fenced in shadow war with the installations below. Site 317701 carried some very sophisticated radars. Far too sophisticated for its apparent purpose. Jamison watched the summaries with absolute concentration.

He had enough.

"Get us out of here. Fast."

Young did not waste time in acknowledging before breaking off the run.

He went to work, then, getting them past the electronic fences that threatened their return to Alaska, some of the densest the Soviets could manage. They dropped, for a brief time, to fifty feet above the tundra.

Jamison was silent, pondering the information they had gathered, knowing it would not yield its secrets until it had been subjected to a full computer analysis. He did not know what they had learned.

But he had a pretty good idea.

Within twenty-four hours General Mann knew, with ineluctable precision, precisely what Stealth had learned: Site 317701 was an extraordinarily advanced beam-type ASAT installation capable of taking out essential chunks of the U.S. military command communications net.

Within the next few hours there was a very quiet, very intense meeting of the Joint Chiefs, chaired by General Mann. From the first, Mann had known in what direction the meeting must go. It was now, he knew, after hours of detailed presentation, very nearly there.

Mann dismissed the last of the analysts. Their questions had been answered. The Joint Chiefs were alone now: Admiral David T. Shaw, USN; General Michael P. Collier, USA; General Malcolm N. Mann, USAF.

Now that they were alone, Shaw was the first to speak.

"So. Where do we go from here?"

"I've got some definite thoughts on that, Dave," Mann said, "but I'd prefer to see where you two are headed first."

"Meaning your notion is pretty far out in left field," Collier said.

Mann nodded.

"The very first thing that we are *not* going to do," Collier said, "is to let those three sites just sit out there. Because if they sit out there, they're going to use them—sooner or later."

"Probably sooner," Shaw said. "At least, if I were them, I would. With this kind of jump they can take out maybe seven-tenths of our command network—at least strategic. All without firing a shot—as far as civilians are concerned."

"I agree," Mann said. "The problem is essentially a political one."

"They'd leave us defenseless," Collier said.

"The beam-ASATs give them an effective no-war war capability," Shaw said ominously. Then he added,

21

in an even more ominous timbre, "A capability we cannot match."

Collier leaned back a bit in his chair, looked at Mann. "Mal," he said, "you've had more time to run this by than we have. I think we're agreed that we have to do something drastic—and quick. Sure as hell they've got a much bigger jump on us in this technology than we thought—intelligence was really sleeping on this one, and the last round of arms talks probably did us in—none of which matters for shit right now. What does matter, I think, and we'd better think about it pretty carefully before we go one thought further, is that if they're going to use this capability—and we have to assume that—how soon will it be, how bad would it be, and can we risk a Cuban scenario over it?"

"Bullshit a Cuban scenario," Shaw said quietly. "Look, Mike, the analyses are clear as crystal. This NSA-type, Jamison, did a good clear analysis of the data. It is clearly a pulsed weapon, take your choice of beam definition, the sites are at altitudes sufficient to minimize beam attenuation factors, and with the analysis of power estimates there is a 95 percent probability of instantaneous satellite kill. They can take out our strategic counters, and then just ask if we wouldn't mind moving along like good little boys. Do you mean to suggest, for even an instant, that we just ask them to disassemble—and then wait to see what they do next?"

"No, I don't," Collier answered. "Someone had to play the devil's advocate."

"Okay," Shaw said, "I understand that. I simply can't imagine the President—or the public—accepting

22

our initiating a shooting war after they'd zapped three-quarters of our strategic command links—and not killed anyone, or fired on American territory, only the satellites—and we'd *lose*."

"So we have no choice," Collier said. "We take them out. Fast. Is the President fully briefed yet, Mal?"

Mann shook his head slowly.

"No. He's not. I took that liberty."

The two men looked at Mann.

"Nor is the Secretary of Defense. I preferred to meet with you first. The President is not prepared to deal with this as it has to be dealt with. And we know it."

There was no sign of dissent.

"I think the Secretary of Defense can be persuaded," Mann said. "I think he can be managed. I don't think the President ever has to know."

D'Alembert was summoned to the office of the Chief of Naval Operations the week before *Adresteia* was to sail on routine patrol. It had been a very early morning meeting. Shaw, the CNO, looked as if he had been up all night. So did the Secretary of Defense.

It had been, for d'Alembert, a rude introduction to the Secretary of Defense, rude information to receive so early in the day.

He remembered.

Remembered the size of the office, the quality of the space in which it enveloped the three men. The hazy light. Remembered the backgrounder, the briefing, the diagrams, the charts, the dust motes in the morning light, the clear drift of the meeting.

D'Alembert was a submarine commander. *Adresteia* was an advanced Trident-type submarine. She carried twenty-four missiles. Ten warheads each. D'Alembert represented the application of that level of ultimate force.

Three missiles would do the job.

He remembered.

D'Alembert found himself in the present. Set his habitual pipe down on the desk.

Fox was still silent, taking it in. Turning it over. Trying to think beyond the single searing thought: *Adresteia* had been ordered to launch. To make a carefully calculated, very specific first strike. Very limited, very precise, against isolated targets. A first strike.

An act of war.

CHAPTER 3

It seemed considerably colder than the ninth circle of
hell on the snow-swept ramp in Nebraska as General
Mann left the warm belly of Looking Glass and
walked toward the waiting courier plane that was to
return him to Washington. His aide walked with him,
the two men hunched against the wind.

The aide spoke quietly despite the whine of the airplane's waiting engines.

"The housekeeping aboard Looking Glass is in
good order, sir."

Mann nodded brusquely in the cold.

"Good. We can't afford the luxury of an untidy
house."

He managed a glance at the aide as they neared the
stairs of the plane.

"No, sir."

Mann hastened up the stairs. The aide followed him
closely, gesturing to the pilot.

With the gesture, the closing door, the airplane
turned them toward the active runway and Washington, their house in order.

Fox lifted his head from his folded hands.

"So we have our orders," he said.

"Presidential."

"They actually expect that we can take out those three sites without starting a full-scale exchange?"

"The decision was made," d'Alembert answered, "to accept that risk."

"But the point of using us is to minimize it."

"The second our birds clear the horizon the lines will go up to Moscow, and the official line will be: The mad submarine commander acting unilaterally."

"The Soviet strategic forces aren't threatened, and the sites are wildly remote."

"Precisely, Charles. So, if you were the Russians, and you knew that in building the beam-ASATs you had pushed the limits, would you respond with anything as irrevocable as strategic retaliation?"

"Probably not."

"Probably not," d'Alembert echoed his executive officer, shifting the emphasis somewhat. "The between-the-lines message, if the Soviets elect to read it that way, will be even clearer: You've gone too far; lie back and let it happen, or we all go up in smoke.

"The cover explanation," the captain continued, "will be that I was fully briefed by the CNO on this newly discovered threat, that three missiles were retargeted to deal with it—to be given first priority in event of war—and that, once at sea, I took matters into my own hands and simply *did* it. We have the independent fire control. If the officers of this boat follow me, yield their keys, we can fire at anything we can target."

Fox considered this carefully.

"The story might wash," he said, "if the Soviets are willing to accept the attack on their ASATs. If."

"Consider, too," d'Alembert said, "that none of this

would ever become public knowledge—it wouldn't be a second Cuban Missile Crisis for the Soviets. The ASATs are so remote that they can easily explain what little would be detected by the outside world. Only they and we would ever know, since it's in the interest of both sides to keep quiet. Very quiet. So the crew is to be transferred to a waiting Spook ship, as per arrangement, then scuttle. New lives, new 'legends' for us, and the corresponding 'legend' for *Adresteia* is that she went down—an accident. And, in the complexities of the turning tale, the legend to be presented to the Soviets is that, in fact, *Adresteia* was sunk by her own for having done what she dared to do."

"Neat, if a little convoluted. It might even work, Captain."

"The planning, Charles, is as detailed as anything I've ever seen. It makes the Holystone and the Grail SSN deployments seem the work of amateurs by comparison."

D'Alembert seemed, for an instant, almost admiring. Fox, outraged at the thought, exploded.

"Jesus fucking Christ, Alex, we are talking about an act of war by an American submarine—*Adresteia*. An unprovoked attack that is legally an act of war, orders or no orders."

D'Alembert answered quietly.

"Not precisely unprovoked."

"It is *still* an act of war."

D'Alembert nodded. "You doubt its legality, Charles, or its wisdom?"

"How . . . ?" Fox began, then broke off. Regained his composure. He seemed, then, to shift his thoughts swiftly, turning to pursue them. He turned, then, to pick up the data in the file d'Alembert had presented

27

him earlier. He seemed to consider it carefully anew, as if thinking new thoughts.

D'Alembert studied Fox sympathetically. He knew full well the doubts Fox felt. Knew that they were only the first. Knew that they would be his, no matter the final outcome, for as long as he lived. Knew how his own had grown until there was no limit to them, until they had led him to where he now sat, controlling them. Fox, d'Alembert knew, was a man capable of near-infinite self-control. If he seemed otherwise now, it was all the more the sign of their dilemma. He watched Fox fight for that control now, fight for it both in and against the data in the papers he studied.

Silently, d'Alembert handed Fox a new folder, its contents written in his own precise hand. He gestured for Fox to read it, studied his reactions as he did so.

Fox turned the pages with deliberation, considering carefully. He betrayed no other emotion. Finally, he placed the folder resignedly back on the desk. Sat down. Buried his head in his hands.

Fox had been handed the whole tangled mess in a single instant, with no real time to think it through. He must choose on instinct. A choice, it seemed, between his captain and his President.

The captain spoke.

"The ancient names, if I recall rightly, are Scylla and Charybdis."

Fox's voice snapped back. "Don't give me fucking mythology, Alex. First you hand me a story of presidential orders to strike against the Soviet Union—and a list of three targets. Now you hand me a list, in your own hand, of three new targets—and all three of those targets are on the North Slope of Alaska."

* * *

The courier plane climbed steadily, its exhaust vapors freezing crystal-hard now, tracing a contrail across the sky.

Mann worked his way steadily through the briefing papers for the day's meetings in the Pentagon. He wore his reading glasses, sipped occasionally at a cup of herb tea—his stomach would tolerate nothing stronger. He would catch a quick nap soon, before they landed. It would be another long day. But not yet.

"Put through a call to Shaw and check on the Fleet exercises," he said to the aide without looking up from his reading. The aide left to place the call as Mann continued to make notes in the margins of a report. He consulted with his watch. Not so very long to Washington.

The aide returned. "ASW exercises in the North Pacific as planned, sir. On schedule. All routine."

"Good. All we have to do is see that it stays that way."

"Yes, sir."

"I'm going to get some sleep."

"Okay, General."

"Tell Auslander we'll be running a little late this morning."

Then the Chairman of the Joint Chiefs of Staff thought better of the message. Smiled to himself.

"No, don't bother. Let him wait."

"I knew something was wrong right from the start, of course. It's hardly standard procedure for the CNO to call in a submarine commander before what's expected to be a routine deterrent patrol. You know that as well as I do. Still, I wasn't overly concerned.

"The moment I stepped into that office and saw Secretary Auslander sitting there with Admiral Shaw—just waiting, it seemed—I knew something was very wrong indeed.

"It didn't take very long to learn what was happening and where it placed *Adresteia*. Shaw did the greater part of the briefing, straight out, no preliminaries. The orders were presidential. I was shown the letter addressed to me with President Elliott's signature—which, Auslander noted, would have to remain with them. What it said, in essence, was that I was to do precisely what I was told to do—though that was asking more of *Adresteia*'s crew than had ever been asked of captain or crew before. I would be told what I needed to know and nothing more. I was. And I wasn't.

"The entire meeting took less than an hour. It seemed a lot longer. The facts about the ASATs and the plain fact that the Russians had attempted to conceal them as installations capable only of threatening Chinese reconnaissance satellites were gone over— enough so that I would appreciate the nature of the threat involved and understand the drastic measures we were being ordered to take. Auslander did a runthrough on the character of the sort of no-war war we risked if we didn't act immediately. He was the Secretary of Defense and he was convincing.

"They were very concerned for the crew personally. Still and all, there was nothing else they could do. We were the only way. They had to rely on us. The President had to rely on us. The United States couldn't do anything this extreme either openly or officially. *Adresteia*'s crew would be made to disappear from the face of the earth, be given new lives, watched over carefully to insure continuing secrecy . . . it was asking a lot. It was asking, they said, everything. We were professionals, we were patriots, and we would do what had to be done. *Adresteia* was the best—the only—weapon for the task at hand, with our independence from Command Control Authority, our invisibility, our invulnerability in the Pacific. . . . They were right.

"Then they went into the details of the transfer to the Company ship after the launch and the plans for the 'hunt' for us for the Russians' benefit, the arrangements for legends for the crew, the oversight security, the entire plan. Charles, the Pentagon has some pretty fine minds available when it wants them, even in something as jealously guarded as this. The thing seemed seamless—or as seamless as anything so desperate could be made to be.

"I had a lot of questions. A world of questions. They answered them. And, in the end, there was that letter in the CNO's hands, and it was from the Commander in Chief. And that was that."

D'Alembert paused for a moment, took a breath, hurried on.

"That was that for a while. For the first two or three days, if I remember rightly, lying awake beside my wife at night—then the questions began to come. They were the kind of questions we're not supposed to ask. At first, I didn't.

"There were men who clearly shadowed every move I made. One faceless sedan or another. Not so obvious as to draw attention—but obvious enough that I noticed. I expected it, in a way, understood it—but it was a presence I couldn't ignore.

"They had said I should contact them if I had any

31

problems, but I didn't—because, frankly, I was afraid.

"Then Mann—General Mann—phoned me person-
ally on the second day after the briefing, just to reassure me and check on me. I can remember every word.
The personal touch, he said, laughing. Then he said
something more—in passing reassurance—that the
NSA ship would be waiting for us when we launched,
everything was arranged. When I said I understood it
was supposed to be a CIA ship he laughed again, said
it was hard to tell ghosts apart in the dark of night—
that Shaw was handling those arrangements.

"But there was something, Charles—the slightest
hesitation, perhaps, or something in the quality of that
laugh—it made me think.

"I had been obsessed, at first, with our chances for
surviving. What it would mean to us personally. Then
I was finally able to reconcile myself to that, to put it
aside. Then I began, for the first time, really, to consider the central question. For *Adresteia* the most detailed part of the plan involved the transfer of the
crew, the arrangements for new lives, and continued
secrecy over the years. For Shaw and Auslander, the
two men who had been with me in that room, and for
Mann, too, the one essential need was to take out
those sites hard, fast, without warning, and to do it
without having done it officially or openly—to maintain absolute deniability. Thus the need to use a
submarine, a Trident submarine, and the need to
place the blame on her officers and crew. Plausible, to
the Soviets, but risky, because the Russians would understand from the first that *Adresteia* was very probably
a scapegoat; but, unless they were willing to confront
the final act of World War Three, they would have to
accept the story.

"The Russians were being told, then, as I said earlier, that they had gone much too far, that the beam-type ASATs concealed in those installations were wildly de-stabilizing—and that the U.S. was determined to maintain stability at any cost. That would be the unequivocal message the instant our missiles were airborne. That would be the inescapable fact of it, and it was the one essential need for Mann, Shaw, and Auslander, the men who actually gave me our orders.

"The need to preserve this crew, it occurred to me, was secondary and, in a number of ways, compromised that need. I came, very, very slowly, to accept the importance of that fact. What got in my way, at first, was that I could not believe that the President, that Spencer Elliott, would condemn us to death. I simply couldn't accept that.

"I tried. I knew I could be wrong—that if it was a matter of national survival a President would have no choice—he would sacrifice the lives of a submarine crew if he had to. It was hard for me to accept, but it was logical. It was possible.

"Still, it bothered me. Something didn't quite fit. The men watching me fit. Mann's phone call fit. But something was *wrong*. I worried at it, and I worried at it. Finally, I found it. I thought the simplest thought of all, the one they had meant me never to find beyond the web of fear and loyalty and pride they had woven for me. It was the letter. Auslander and Shaw had waved that letter in my face, with the President's signature, carefully explaining that they had to keep it to guarantee the President's deniability. I had been so impressed, so off-guard, that I had bought it. It was impressive. It felt right.

"But it wasn't right."

Fox raised an eyebrow, listening.

"It wasn't right at all. If the President had to give an order which had to be absolutely, utterly secret, if he had to be assured absolute deniability—how in hell could he risk handing a letter over to the Joint Chiefs? In a world full of Xerox machines? When he had to know damn well that the interests of the Joint Chiefs didn't always coincide with his own?"

D'Alembert shook his head.

"No way, Charles. No way. That letter was a forgery."

As the plane that carried General Mann flared for a landing at Andrews Air Force Base, William Fraser Auslander, the Secretary of Defense, waited anxiously in the study adjoining his office. The phone rang with the message that Mann had landed, was on his way. He returned to the vigil he kept beside the fireplace.

Auslander was easily the least willing of the principal participants in the affair. He had been carried by the Joint Chiefs for the simple reason that they were the military authorities, and this matter involving ASATs and *Adresteia* was overwhelmingly a matter best addressed by expert military judgment. He had been carried for the even simpler reasons that he was, in some ways, weak. He had been overwhelmed, he thought, and began to regret it.

Auslander worked for a bit at lighting his pipe, his habitual lawyerly gesture, the bid for time, if only from himself.

He regretted it. It no longer mattered. He was committed.

* * *

Adresteia moved silently in the darkness of the Pacific, five hundred meters beneath the surface, steady on her course, reaching out from the coast. She moved steadily indeed, for no mere surface disturbance reaches five hundred meters beneath the surface. Nor does light penetrate. Sound prevails. Pressure, both constant and modulated. Constant pressure *Adresteia*'s alloyed steel hull could withstand. Modulated pressure her sonar could sense at a distance. Darkness and the many-textured pressures of the Pacific prevailed, and these were things *Adresteia*'s designers had well understood.

D'Alembert was, in a word, desperate. He had considered how to bring Fox this far. He did not know any way to bring him the final distance. Fox, he knew, would have to do it himself.

Fox was a good officer. A very good officer. If he were not, d'Alembert would have had no hope, would never have permitted his doubts to bring him to this point.

D'Alembert cleaned his pipe, waiting. It was a ceremonial act, and he knew it. The pipe was a bad habit. He could no longer afford bad habits. He could no longer afford mistakes. He put the piece of carved wood away.

D'Alembert stood, looked at the photograph that was the room's only ornament. An abstraction of light and shadow. Something to focus on.

He glanced down at Fox, who still sat on the edge of the bed. D'Alembert sat down beside him, the two men perhaps six inches apart, staring at the steel bulkhead. D'Alembert was a submariner, a captain, accustomed in his particular professional way to the meaning of silences. He would wait this one out. He would wait out the others as well.

Finally, Fox spoke.

"Alex, how long have you known?"

"A week."

"How long have you known what you'd do?"

D'Alembert briefly considered the seamless character of the wall.

"Known? Four days."

"Yeah."

D'Alembert waited.

He had waited for what had seemed a similar small eternity when he had put the question to his wife the night before *Adresteia* was to sail.

He had considered carefully—very carefully—before telling her what was on his mind. It was a serious violation of security to do so—but if he was right, if the Joint Chiefs had taken matters into their own hands, there had already been a serious breach of security. He had to stop it. And Morgan had to know.

First, though, before he could attempt to act, he needed confirmation of his judgment, needed reassurance that his reasons were sound. He couldn't possibly embark on the course he now contemplated if he in any way doubted his decision—and Morgan was an intelligent woman whose own judgment was to be taken seriously.

Still, it had taken him some time to bring the matter up for discussion.

They had tucked Jennifer and Joshua into bed, kissed them good night. Saying good-bye to the children before every patrol was always a trial for him—

this time even more than most. Morgan and he returned to the living room for a glass of wine before going up to bed.

There was a great roaring fire in the fireplace. "Sure you don't want to wake them up early in the morning before you leave?" Morgan asked.

He took a sip from his glass. "No," he said quietly. "Let them sleep."

She had nodded in understanding. The patrols were long, sixty days or thereabouts, and the leaving was always hard. Hard on her. Hard on him. Hard on the children.

"They'll be off for Christmas vacation in a few days," she said. "They're looking forward to it."

He nodded. She must sense, he thought, his unusual degree of concern—his anxiety. But she would never ask him the reason for it, knowing that it must have to do with the patrol to come.

"Why don't you and the kids go on a real vacation this year?" he asked suddenly.

"What do you mean?" she asked, sensing in the tone of the unexpected suggestion that something was wrong.

"Something different. Instead of staying around the house during the holidays."

She brushed back a long strand of her dark hair. The gray of her eyes reflected the firelight back at him. "Can we afford it?" she asked as casually as she could, still sensing that the idea was anything but casual, that he was leading up to something.

"Why not?" he said, his heart clearly not in it.

It had long been an unspoken understanding between them that they never said how much they would miss one another—not before he left. After a patrol, when he was finally safely back, it was bearable—but not before.

Casually, it seemed, she lifted her glass, looking at the firelight through the crystal. "Something bothering you?"

He took a deep breath.

"Yes."

"Want to talk about it?"

He shook his head slowly, tried to manage a smile, however half-hearted. "Not in the least. But we have to."

She looked at him.

"I was in Washington a few days ago," he said slowly, finding his way, "to meet with the CNO and the Secretary of Defense. That's why I haven't been able to sleep since."

She listened in silence that night as he told her what he knew—the men watching, the call from Mann, his final crucial doubt about the presidential letter. She had listened in silence, asking few questions. Listening and thinking.

It had been a long wait while she thought, while he waited for her to speak. Her hair, he noticed, was still a bit damp from the shower she had taken earlier. She sat seemingly motionless, knowing their lives were changed forever. He guessed at her thoughts in a thousand ways, waiting.

Finally, she spoke.

"What do we do to stop them?"

In that question he had his last doubts answered. The nightmare was real, not imagined.

If it was real, it could be fought.

"I've been trying to find a way to reach the President," he said. "But I don't know who I can trust."

"Devlin?" she asked immediately.

"I thought of that," he said. "If I can trust anyone I can trust Devlin. But I don't know if I can trust anyone—and I can't afford to be wrong. In any case, he's on an inspection tour of operations in the Mediterranean and won't be back for a couple of days yet. If I try and reach him, it would probably be noticed."

She nodded.

"What then?" she asked, knowing he had been thinking the thing over for days.

"I think I know a way," he said. "But it will be very dangerous. And it could fail."

She looked into the fire before speaking again. "Is it worth a chance?"

He managed a slight laugh.

"There isn't much to lose, is there?"

There was no need to answer that question.

They talked all night. There were sticking points, a number of them, and they could not all be resolved. They were, in a number of ways, outmatched—and they knew it. Still, they had to try.

He had left her in the hour before dawn, leaving for the base where *Adresteia* lay in waiting. They had kissed a last time in the doorway, and he had left her. They were both alone then.

He was alone still, with his executive officer, waiting. Fox looked at him.

"Do we need to discuss legalities any further, Captain?"

D'Alembert smiled at his friend's question.

"I don't think so."

"I really haven't time to think this through."

"We don't have it, Charles."

"Alex, I've just never been guilty of disobeying an order before. Any order. Let alone treason."

"I haven't given you any orders, Charles, and I won't. Not until you decide. The choice is yours."

Fox stiffened. His voice stiffened as well. He was coming hard and suddenly to himself and to his decision.

"Captain," he said, "the issues involved here are complex, and I can't resolve them. What I have to decide is whether to trust your judgment absolutely, above all else, and turn this ship against her own government—or to defy you."

D'Alembert stared at the bulkhead.

"Yes."

Fox paused for half an instant.

"Very well, Captain. We will defy them together."

CHAPTER 4

The United States' Attack Submarine SSN *Orcus* sailed the Arctic Ocean.

Four thousand meters above the Pole Abyssal Plain, five hundred meters below the ice, she hunted a Russian missile submarine.

It was a game, of course.

The game's first object was to trail the enemy submarine without detection. The second was to close within kill range undetected. Less desirably, the object of the exercise was to close within kill range despite being detected.

For the Russian vessel the object was simple. Avoid detection. If detected, lose the hunter.

The informal exercise had a serious purpose. A number of such purposes. Mutual deterrence was based in great part on the statistical invulnerability of the strategic missile submarines of both sides. As long as that balance remained in favor of the missile submarines' undetectability, neither side was greatly concerned with the detection of an individual vessel.

The skippers liked to match wits.

Russell Hansen, captain of the *Orcus*, liked very much to match wits with the opposition. He was a professional who enjoyed his work.

The Soviet missile submarine had, by ill chance, brushed within a sonar screen based on the ocean floor as she made her way north to the polar ice cap. Now that the Soviets had finally improved the quiet-running capabilities of their boats it happened less often than it once did but, still, it happened.

Now *Orcus* sought her out.

Few other Soviet subs were currently fixed on the war charts. Hansen hoped to position this one.

Orcus was smaller, faster, deeper-diving, silent as death beneath the ice, but it was no small task. Each of their advantages was but incremental.

A black-hulled shape in the blackness beneath the polar ice, *Orcus* searched.

With Fox's decision finally made, the captain and his executive officer turned as one to the task of defying the will of the Joint Chiefs. D'Alembert had, in the final days before *Adresteia* sailed, formed the nucleus of the stratagem to be employed and had, in sending his wife off to Switzerland on a "vacation," taken the first step.

Both men knew well that they were in a desperately risky situation. *Adresteia*, most recently launced of the Trident submarines, was virtually undetectable in the vastness of the Pacific, and she was formidably armed, both offensively and defensively. The problem, however, was not how to fight, it was how to stop the attack on the Soviet ASATs—an attack d'Alembert and Fox were now both convinced was planned in ignorance of the President, and an attack that might mean World War Three.

The problem, then, was how to bring *Adresteia*'s force effectively to bear. And the problem, too, was how to hold the officers and men of *Adresteia* united in a time of tested loyalties. In addition, they had to work quickly.

It was a long day and a longer night while Fox and d'Alembert evolved a detailed strategy. Then, after the briefest of rests, d'Alembert summoned the ship's senior officers to a meeting in the wardroom.

Auslander toyed with the ice in his glass, took another sip of the drink. It was late. He should have left for home over an hour ago. But the massive office in the Pentagon was his second home, a private one if he so chose, if the day's work was done.

The day's work was done. The official and the unofficial. Mann had come and gone in his expected storm of energy. There were no problems yet, though some could be expected. It was proving troublesome to maintain the necessary level of secrecy. Mann, however, anticipated everything, and Mann, Auslander had noted very early in their acquaintance, was quite efficient at eliminating problems before they had a chance to happen. The small task force in the North Pacific would have no hint of the real reason for its exercises, would think them simply maneuvers.

So Mann didn't particularly care for him. Who really expected the Chairman of the Joint Chiefs to respect the Secretary of Defense—except, perhaps in the press releases where the usual deference was made to the civilian officeholder's extraordinary energy and leadership ability?

Auslander was essentially an administrator, a manager. An able one. Elliott had appointed him to keep the bureaucracy in check and he had attempted mightily to do just that—with, he felt, some notable success.

He poured himself another drink. Yes, some notable success.

If Mann and the other Chiefs found him insufficiently "tough," not military enough, let them think so. He could show them if it ever came to that. He could hold the line with them on the ASATs, do what had to be done, even if it meant keeping it from the President. *Adresteia*, though. . . . He still hoped to make a case for *Adresteia*. The military, he thought, was sometimes a little too eager to find the necessary courage to sacrifice its own.

It was time to go home. His wife would be waiting. They really should try to put in an appearance at the Iranian ambassador's tonight. If there was time. It was already late.

Adresteia's senior officers gathered in the wardroom. In addition to d'Alembert and Fox, the group consisted of Stewart, the ship's engineering officer; Thomson, the weapons officer; and Michaels, the electronics officer. Stewart, Thomson, and Michaels had no notion why the captain had called this meeting, but they knew that the captain and the executive officer had been in conference for much of the preceding twenty-four hours—that something serious was about to happen. A submarine presents a very intimate space to its officers and crew, even if it is as massive as a Trident submarine. There are few secrets. If they are to survive they must be jealously guarded.

The five men settled themselves at the table, made small talk, helped themselves to coffee. D'Alembert eased his chair back a bit from the table and spoke into the silence that awaited him.

"Gentlemen, *Adresteia* is going to target three missiles on the North Slope of Alaska. She will then tie into NavSynch 7 and inform General Mann and the Joint Chiefs that unless the sum of twenty-five million dollars is secretly and expeditiously transferred to Swiss accounts we will launch those missiles."

A frantic silence followed this terse declaration. The three astonished officers looked, for a moment, from d'Alembert to Fox, unable for an instant to fathom whether this were some joke, and they should laugh, or something else entirely—and they should laugh. Neither the expression of the captain nor that of his second-in-command suggested laughter, and in the half-second that the impulse had formed it likewise vanished. A longer shade of silence filled the next few seconds.

Thomson, the weapons officer, the youngest, was the first to venture a reaction.

"That would be insane."

"On the contrary, Thomson," d'Alembert answered him, "it is the closest attempt we can manage to regain sanity. The form of our madness is quite different. It was presented to me, directly enough, by the Secretary of Defense and the Chief of Naval Operations. It was presented to me sealed with a presidential seal, scrupulously defended, carefully justified. I am willing to wager my life and my honor that that seal is false. I am willing to wager my soul that this is madness and must be prevented.

"We are going to choose between two forms of madness, gentlemen, because that is the only choice we have. And we are going to begin that choice right now."

D'Alembert held each man's gaze in turn.

"Mr. Fox, explain for us all the choice we have before us."

D'Alembert leaned back. Watching. Judging. Attempting to direct *Adresteia*'s course with the force of his will alone as *Adresteia* sailed on and Fox began the recital of the dimension of their dilemma.

"The skipper asked me to speak because I've been going through what you're going through now for the last twenty-four hours. I've probably asked most of the questions you want to ask—need to ask. Let me begin at the beginning. My beginning. The first thing I knew was when we received a message off the command net just before we submerged. . . ."

Spencer Elliott, the President of the United States, walked the White House grounds in sleeplessness. He was tired. Restless. The interval before the convening of the new Congress was proving far too brief as he labored to prepare new legislation, met with his advisers and congresspeople. It was now the second half of his first term of office. If he was going to win a second term there had better be some dramatically sound progress on the domestic front. The international agreements forged in the first two years were well and necessary and good and provided an aura of leadership, but international affairs seldom mattered very much when it came time for people to vote.

The lights fell in cold form on the lawn. He turned his steps toward the garden. Some paperwork. His wife. Then sleep. Perhaps.

Fox told them of the ASATs and their orders, the captain's first doubts. D'Alembert looked on, put in an occasional word, judged reactions. Fox spoke simply and well. Frequently the eyes of one or another of the men would find their way to d'Alembert's own. D'Alembert held them.

Fox explored the possibility, the very real possibility, that such a strike as they had been ordered to carry out would provoke a war rather than prevent it. That, naturally enough, a strategist's priorities would favor risking war rather than risk the possibility of being put in a position of not being able to fight one, if it came, on an equal footing—the "no-war war" scenario. That the priorities, the perspective, of the Joint Chiefs and, by inclusion, Auslander, would perforce be those of a strategist.

"The priorities of a civilian, however, functioning as a civilian, might well be less 'daring.' The President is, of course, a civilian, and we are meant to be directly accountable to that civilian leadership.

"But all we have," Fox concluded his lengthy summary, "is a piece of paper shown to the skipper."

D'Alembert let Fox's words sink in for a few moments before he leaned forward, resting his elbows on the table, and spoke.

"We all know something about Spencer Elliott, I think," he said. "None of us knows him personally, but, still, we know something about the man. The first question to ask ourselves, it seems to me, is this: How likely is it that Elliott actually gave such an order?"

Thomson was again the first to respond.

"Skipper, I don't see how that question is any of our business. The President is the Commander in Chief. Admiral Shaw and Secretary Auslander serve at his pleasure. We have no reason not to believe that they were relaying orders directly from the President. It just isn't our job to ask questions. Would we debate an order to retaliate? Ask to speak to the President personally? If it came through proper channels, we'd carry it out. Without asking questions. We have no reason not to believe our orders are legitimate."

"He's got a point, Captain," Stewart said. "There's a line, I think, between doubting the authenticity of our orders and doubting their authenticity because we don't care for the orders."

There seemed to be some agreement, attempting to solidify itself around their perception of duty. D'Alembert had to force them to form a different perspective on their duty.

"I agree with you a hundred percent," d'Alembert said quietly. "There is a crucial distinction between doubting an order and doubting it because you don't like it. What I'm suggesting is that there are substantial reasons for doubting this order, although they may not be immediately apparent. They may even be fairly subtle. But they are very real. Trust me enough on this to hear my reasoning through. Fair enough?"

There was no sign of disagreement, though there was a certain uneasiness. No one wanted to be taken where d'Alembert sought to lead them.

D'Alembert did not hesitate.

"Put yourself in General Mann's position. The ASATs are out there. They are capable of taking out a large portion of the military command network without an actual attack on the United States. The very fact that they are there is evidence of bad faith.

"There is no effective defense. If the command network is destroyed, then a good portion of American strategic capacity is effectively neutralized. That is an

48

intolerable situation to a military commander. Absolutely intolerable.

"What do you do? If you go to the President you know that he will in all probability attempt a diplomatic approach of some sort. You know he's not going to simply take your recommendation at face value, just do what you tell him has to be done. Yet you know that the one thing you have going for you is that the Russians don't know you know—yet. If the President uses any sort of conventional diplomatic approach—no matter how firm the line is—you lose that advantage. You may, in fact, provoke the very thing you fear most.

"Make sense?"

There was general, if at first hesitant, agreement that it did.

"That, then," d'Alembert resumed, "is the first reason for suspicion. The next is more invidious. Charles outlined for you the arrangements for the rendezvous with the CIA ship. The plan, we're told, is that we're to surface at the designated coordinates in the North Pacific, in open waters, and transfer the crew to the waiting ship. Then we scuttle. Then the Russians, in the scenario offered us, are told we were hunted down by a U.S. ASW force and sunk with all hands. Then we're all relocated, given new identities, and watched over to make sure no one ever breathes a word that might reach the public or the Russians."

D'Alembert took a sip of coffee.

"This is the least probable part of the plan if it is only considered carefully. By far. We can target the ASATs. We can launch at a low trajectory and destroy them before they can react. The U.S. can then tell the

Russians that *Adresteia* did it on her own. Then comes the crunch. Do the Russians accept the explanation as offered, feel sufficiently reassured—and fail to retaliate? If there's going to be a real chance of that happening, if the Russians are going to accept it, the U.S. is going to have to go some distance to show good faith in its story. 'Destroying' *Adresteia* is number one on that list."

D'Alembert paused for effect.

"That destruction *must* be credible and it *must* be kept secret. None of this will bear close public scrutiny. The ASATs are remote, so they can be explained away as an earthquake or testing or an accident or any combination of the above. The Russians can handle that easily. The U.S. can almost as easily say that *Adresteia* exploded internally and sank—though that will be more tricky. It could happen. It would be embarrassing, awkward, unpleasant—but not unmanageable. There is no reason to connect the two events. Only American or Soviet radars could track the missiles on a highly depressed trajectory, and there would be few of those. All, then, manageable.

"What is *not* manageable, gentlemen, what cannot be risked is that the Soviets be confronted with the fact that they have been deceived, that we did not fire without orders. They will suspect that, yes. They will be able to put aside that suspicion only if the U.S. clearly and unequivocally demonstrates the sincerity of its story. Dramatically. Destroys its own submarine and its own crew. That, gentlemen, is 'good faith.'

"Now. To the telling point. If you were General Mann, any one of the Joint Chiefs, if you were the one responsible for our orders . . . could you accept the risk of having one hundred and fifty men alive who are living proof of your bad faith—and, presumably, their families? Could you provide covers that were infallible? Guarantee nothing would go wrong in the elaborate transfer? No one would make a mistake, have second thoughts? A crew of one hundred and fifty men?

"How in hell are you supposed to do that?"

D'Alembert glared at them now.

"How?" he demanded. "You don't. That's how. You make them disappear. Forever."

D'Alembert slumped back in his seat as if drained. There was some tense fussing with coffee cups. Michaels rose to fill his.

D'Alembert had always run *Adresteia* as a close boat. He was risking that now, risking everything in an attempt to win unanimity. He and Fox had known from the first that they had to have the others solidly behind them or they would fail utterly.

They must not fail.

D'Alembert spoke again from the depths of his chair.

"I'm not asking you to take this on faith. The people that are asking you to take it on faith are Shaw and Auslander and the Joint Chiefs. We know that much.

"What I am asking is your trust. Primarily I am asking for your trust in your own good judgment. I don't have all the answers. Neither does Charles. In fact, we both have a lot of questions of our own.

"Maybe we can find the answer together. I'll tell you one thing with absolute certainty. We are either going to find the answer together or we are going to die together. Soon."

* * *

It was early morning. Precisely 0600. Time for General Mann to run his morning five kilometers.

Mann circled the track at an even pace, a fair turn of speed for a man of sixty. A fair turn of speed for many a much younger man. The limousine waited patiently beside the cinder track. There was frost on the grass in the infield.

It had been nearly ten years since Mann last flew a fighter plane, an F-15. He had had to stay hard then. Staying hard had saved his life a few times in F-4s, pulling some very hard G's when the SAMs were out. It was a losing battle now, he was growing older.

He ran harder.

D'Alembert bothered him. He was the only thing, the only one that did, really. It was a waste, in a way. Mann had studied his records carefully. D'Alembert was a good officer—a very good officer. It was unfair and there was some measure of risk in so using him. The risk was, he felt, minimal. D'Alembert would carry out any task he set himself, no matter how difficult.

It was unfair, yes, but life was unfair. Which was a pretty poor excuse.

He needed no excuse. He had sent men to die before. It had been necessary. He had risked it himself. He had been as close as you could get and come back.

He slowed for one lap. Ran easily.

D'Alembert bothered him. Mann ran till the pain came, then held the pace—went the distance he assigned himself.

The driver was waiting.

"This, gentlemen, is the plan."

Fox spoke now. D'Alembert peered over the coffee

mug he held before his steam-masked face, sipping thoughtfully, listening.

"We have twenty-four hours to think this thing through before absolutely committing ourselves. During that time we will do three things: First, we will begin a high-speed distance/evasive run, leaving our assigned course, losing ourselves. Second, we will prepare the junior officers and control room crew for what we are about to do. Third, the weapons officer will retarget the three necessary missiles on the specified coordinates on the North Slope.

"All these things are best done immediately. The missiles cannot be fired without the four necessary firing keys, so the preparations do not absolutely commit us. We hope, of course, that it won't come to that. If it does, we've lost. Still, this is not a situation in which we can bluff our way out. We have to be prepared to act.

"What we propose is based on a simple premise. If we are right, the President does not know of our orders. But there is no way for us to contact the President except through the military command net and, under the circumstances, we can't accept the authenticity of any such communication received through that net. We have to stop this thing on our own. If we are right, and the Joint Chiefs and the Secretary of Defense are the authors of this mission, then their one vulnerable point is their need for absolute and complete secrecy. They cannot risk exposure.

"That, we hope is our hole card."

Stewart took in the captain and the exec together. "I think I'm beginning to get your drift. It might work."

D'Alembert answered him. "We think we have a chance. A good chance. If we call their bluff, defy them, refuse the mission, demand a ransom of twenty-five million dollars and the abandonment of the mission—or we take out the North Slope and stir up the biggest investigation in history—they'll have to yield. We deny them the ability to maintain their cover story, both for the mission and for themselves. Without that ability, they fail.

"If we succeed, if we leave this boat with some measure of security, we have a chance of surviving. We officers will have to relocate and live our lives out in exile abroad. The money will give us the means to do that. We will maintain frequent contact to make it impossible for anyone to attempt to 'hit' all of us at once—any attempt, any false move, and we go public—and they'll know that. We have to count on their knowing that. I'll also want to put a couple of men ashore, if they agree to our demands, before we return to base—for some insurance.

"It's risky. Very risky. But there's no safe path open to us. We have to take our chances as we see fit."

Thomson looked up from the table.

"If it doesn't work, Captain? What then?"

"If they try to hunt us down, they compound the chances of their own exposure. If all else fails, we launch. That will take some lives—we can't avoid that, though we're going to target largely deserted areas, and they'll have warning to evacuate if the Joint Chiefs give it to them. They know our capabilities. What would be their chances of even finding us?"

"Piss-poor, Skipper, but they might try," Stewart said. "It would only get them in deeper, I'll grant you that, but if they feel strongly enough about the need to destroy those ASATs their way, they might be foolish enough to try."

Fox spoke up.

"If they try, they'll fail. *Adresteia* is too good and the Pacific is too big. They won't even know where to start looking. We could be anywhere. They'll never find us."

"Okay, let's be realistic," Michaels said. "What's to stop them from using another boat—or an alternate means altogether—on the ASATs?"

"We gave that a lot of thought," d'Alembert said. "We're convinced the only weapons system that makes sense, considering the need both for a clean, hard hit and absolute deniability, is an SSBN. It would have to be a Trident boat. They'll be in a very narrow bind if we defy them. If we succeed, and survive, with financial resources enough to buy some security for ourselves, we threaten them with exposure if they turn to other means later."

"A deterrent situation," Thomson observed.

"Exactly," d'Alembert said. "I expect that a deterrent situation is something that a General Mann or an Admiral Shaw is infinitely capable of appreciating.

"Look," he said, "we're talking details. We can talk details later. What matters, right now, is that we decide where we stand. There is no way out for us. No matter what we do, we stand an excellent chance of winding up dead. If we live, I, for one, want to be able to live with myself.

"Are you with me or against me?"

CHAPTER 5

They were with him.

Thank God.

The chief officers separated now, Stewart and Thomson to begin the retargeting of the missiles, Michaels to work out the details of the communications codes, Fox to begin preparing the junior officers.

The crew, as a whole, must not know—their survival, in the long run, depended on ignorance, their not presenting a threat to the Joint Chiefs. There were those though, who must know—the control room crew, the junior officers, a few others. That, too, was a chance they would have to take.

D'Alembert took the con.

"Any recent contact, sonar?"

"Negative, Captain."

"Diving officer?"

"Sir?"

"Give me five fifty."

"Aye, aye, Skipper, five five zero."

Adresteia started down, seeking still greater depths, taking the greater weight of the ocean above her. The greater pressure meant they might run fast with less chance of detection. The risk of propeller cavitation was reduced with greater depth, greater pressure. The chances of thermal layers or deep scattering layers intervening to refract or reflect what little sound they made were likewise improved. The increased pressure, enemy though it was, was also an ally.

"Five five zero, Captain. Steady as she goes."

"Very well, Warren."

D'Alembert studied the navigational display that dominated the forward extremity of the control room. It displayed a wide range of integrated information: submerged mountain ranges and valleys, available information on the sonar "nets" emplaced in various parts of the world's oceans, estimates of sound propagation patterns . . . any data that *Adresteia's* computers could present could be presented there in graphic form.

"Helm, come to two eight three. Give me flank speed."

"Aye, aye, sir, two eight three. Calling for flank speed."

Instantly, *Adresteia's* seventeen thousand tons began silently to accelerate as the helmsmen rolled them to the new course. D'Alembert watched the display as their speed steadily built. The helmsmen rolled them level. *Adresteia* continued to build speed.

"Gentlemen," D'Alembert addressed the control room crew, "we are going to do some very serious distance running for the next twenty-four hours. I want a *very* sharp watch. Understood?"

He was understood.

Admiral Shaw and General Collier held a brief working session that day, the better to evaluate the current state of progress. Their chief aides remained beside them as they alternately worked and lunched in Collier's office. It had been a profitable meeting.

"Okay, Dave," Shaw said. "So the destroyer is finalized. It'll be flanking the task force as a whole, but wide, and in good position to move when *Adresteia* surfaces. Am I right on that?"

"Right." The CNO hesitated a moment, then said, "The thing that bothers me just a little is that we have to use a destroyer for the job. I'm not entirely happy with that—it just isn't optimal—but, under the circumstances, there should be no problem."

"Why not entirely happy?"

Shaw put down his sandwich. "You know something about antisubmarine warfare, right?"

"A little. It's not exactly my specialty—I've seen damn few submarines in the middle of a battlefield."

"Right. Well, the long and the short of it are that a submarine, especially a Trident boat, is very hard to locate. With a Trident, in fact, it can be next to impossible. In almost all instances, the signal level generated by the submarine is less than ambient levels in the ocean. Even with advanced signal-processing techniques, it can be almost impossible. There are a lot of complexities in hunting a sub, especially a Trident. The only rational approach, if you have to do it one-to-one, is with an attack submarine—preferably an *Orcus*-class boat. A surface ship, any surface ship, is just too damn noisy and inflexible."

"But we're stuck with a surface ship," Collier said, "because that's what D'Alembert expects to be in the area when he surfaces for the 'transfer.'"

"Exactly." Shaw took a bite out of his sandwich.

"Is it really a problem? We know his location, of

course, because we told him to be there. All the destroyer has to do is wait."

"Pretty much. The destroyer won't be in sensor range when *Adresteia* surfaces, not really, and if his sonar does get anything in the passive mode, d'Alembert will be expecting a high-speed ship anyway, so that alone won't alarm him." The CNO sipped at his coffee, washing down another bite. "We have to be very careful, though, that his sonar doesn't get anything worth looking at. If his man gets a good signature, identifies the ship, he's going to know something really weird is happening. If I were in his position . . ." Shaw hesitated, "I don't know how I'd react. I'm not a submariner, Dave, but his reaction time, even if he's taken completely off guard, can be pretty damn quick."

"Then we have to deal with him in the same way as the ASATs—hard and clean."

"Definitely. Absolutely. It definitely has to be clean. The destroyer can stand well off and still do the job. I'd prefer to use the ideal weapon, and an attack submarine is an ideal weapon—but not here. No, not here—same reason I ruled out shadowing *Adresteia* when she left port. D'Alembert is just too damn good, and so is his crew. He used to command an attack sub before he moved to this command—*Orcus*, in fact, the lead boat. No, he knows the tricks. If he got wind of an attack sub on his trail when he left port it would start him adding it all up and we'd have lost the whole thing. No, we'll stick to the plan," Shaw concluded, as much to himself as to Collier. "The task force being in that area on exercises will muddy the waters for d'Alembert anyway."

Collier finished his sandwich. "How many people do we have in the know at this point in time?"

"My people? How many, Jack?"

The aide answered without consulting any list.

"Eleven."

"Good," Collier said. "Very good. That's really tight under the circumstances."

"You're telling me."

"I know. I've only got six on my end, but considering I don't have to make the sort of arrangements you do, it's a lot simpler. Mann's end, though, coordination, has the potential of getting ragged."

"Agreed," Shaw said. "That's one reason I'm glad it's someone like Mann."

"Likewise."

The aides, then, acting on some invisible signal, began to gather up the papers. Collier finished his coffee, placed the cup on its saucer.

"Dave?" he asked.

"Yeah."

"Mind if I get just a little bit personal?"

"Shoot," the CNO answered.

"What about d'Alembert?"

"What about him?"

"Your being the one to give him the orders—Navy man to Navy man. He'll do the job."

"D'Alembert?" Shaw laughed. "Hell, yes, d'Alembert is one tough bastard when he needs to be. He'll do the job."

"No, that's not what I mean. I mean your doing it to him."

"Oh. That."

"Yes. That."

"Precisely how do you mean?" Shaw asked.

"Well . . . we've both been through this sort of thing in general—it comes with the territory. This, though, is worse in some ways."

Shaw glanced out the window. "I know what you mean," he said.

"Is it any different?"

Shaw thought for a moment, then answered.

"No, not for me, anyway. It's the same. Exactly the same. I feel like three-day-old shit."

"Guess I shoudn't have asked. I apologize."

"No. There's nothing to apologize for. As you said, it comes with the territory."

The Soviet submarine that ran deep beneath the polar ice sought, above all else, to avoid detection. A ballistic missile submarine, an infinitely less sophisticated counterpart to *Adresteia,* her mission was deterrence. She was to lose herself in the Arctic Ocean. If war were to come she would find herself, loose her twenty-four missiles on American targets. Deterrence. Above all else she sought to avoid detection.

They ran slowly now, less than ten knots, suspended in the slowly moving night that was their ocean. Ran silently. Were silent. Thought silent.

Orcus searched for them, though they did not know it. More than a hundred miles separated them. *Orcus* ran with some speed, making twenty-five knots. She could run faster, much faster, but Hansen's experience thought this speed best for his present purpose. He had only a crude notion of where the Soviet sub might be. He had to strike a compromise between speed, sweeping a good deal of ocean, and running more slowly, which would enable *Orcus* to listen more effectively. Periodically they would stop, listening hard, then move on, still searching.

Orcus was an attack submarine, latest of the type. She could run far faster than the Russian missile submarine. Even more importantly, she could run more silently. Her one design goal was to hunt submarines. That was Hansen's task. They were optimized for it. Still, it was a big ocean.

D'Alembert was sleeping soundly when the intercom summoned him awake.

"Yes."

"Michaels, Skipper. Am I disturbing you?"

"I've run through all phases of our projected link with the com net and I don't see any glitches. The existing computer codes will take care of our needs."

"Good. I thought so. Any luck with the other?"

"Sorry, Skipper. I tried. There's no way we can tie directly into a presidential command link and be absolutely sure. If the com net link computers are programmed to shunt us off on a side track . . . there's no way for us to know."

D'Alembert stifled a yawn. "I expected that."

"I know, Skipper. So did I. I thought it was worth a try, anyway—the frustrating thing is that any communication received over the executive command channel would have to be from the President—but there's no way to work it the other way, to reach him."

D'Alembert nodded grimly to himself, asked, "How are you on sleep, Michaels?"

"A little behind, I guess."

"Get some. Then relieve Fox."

"Okay, Skipper."

D'Alembert switched off the intercom. Michaels was a good man. If he said there was absolutely no way they could get a sure link to the President, then there wasn't any. They were indeed in the middle. He keyed the control room on the intercom.

"Fox here, Captain."

"How are we, Charles?"

"No contacts, Skipper. No shadows."

"Good. I didn't see how they could have managed it, anyway."

"Good to know, though, isn't it?"

"That it is. The birds, Charles?"

"Two down. One to go."

"Tell me when three is ready or have Stewart tell me."

"Right."

D'Alembert switched off the intercom again. He lay back on the bunk, stared at the ceiling. No, there was no way that they could have effectively anticipated his defying orders. If the possibility had occurred to them at all, it had been faint, a risk they had to accept. It had seemed their least problem, their slightest risk.

Within thirty-seven hours they would learn it was their greatest.

Auslander, too, failed to sleep. He lay awake for over an hour before conceding defeat, leaving the bedroom quietly so as not to disturb his wife. He went downstairs to his study, closed the door.

Tomorrow—today—they would finalize the arrangements for dealing with the President. An explanation would be necessary when *Adresteia* launched on the ASATs. It had better be good. It had better be flawless. Elliot was no man's fool.

* * *

Adresteia ran swift and silent, distancing herself from the continent. She ran deep. Nearly three days and two thousand miles from home.

"Mr. Fox, I have something on the lateral."

The lateral line was an array of transducers running the length of the outer pressure hull to port and starboard. It was a variety of passive sonar device, one that listened to long-wave sounds, screened them electronically, sifted them through the ship's computers. The lateral furnished distant warning.

"What have you got, sonar?"

"Only the lateral has him."

"Helm, take her down another hundred. Ahead one-third."

"Aye, aye, sir."

Each of *Adresteia*'s helmsmen held a small joystick that functioned like the ones in high-performance aircraft. It extended from the armrest of their seats and controlled the diving planes in both unison and differential action as well as the ship's rudders. The new arrangement offered a more maneuverable submarine than the wheel arrangement it superseded, and maneuverability was vital. For a vessel of one hundred seventy meters and seventeen thousand tons, *Adresteia* was astonishingly maneuverable.

They descended quickly, the diving officer making the necessary slight adjustment in ballast. They were soon at a new equilibrium, six hundred fifty meters beneath the surface.

"Sonar?"

"Very distant, Mr. Fox, but getting nearer. He's at my outer range now . . . surface vessel, I think . . . seems slow. . . ."

"All stop."

"All stop."

Fox waited.

"Definitely surface, Mr. Fox. Freighter or tanker . . . tanker, I believe . . . I don't have enough data for a signature."

"Keep tracking him."

"Aye, aye, sir."

Fox considered their position on the tactical/navigational display.

"Helm, ready to come to two seven five."

"Aye, aye, sir, ready to come to two seven five."

"Ahead one-third. Let's stay on our tiptoes for just a bit."

Half an hour passed.

"Anything, sonar?"

"Lost him for sure, Mr. Fox."

"Come to two four nine. Give me flank speed. Take her up to five zero zero proximate."

It had never been anything but a tanker and Fox knew it. They all knew it. Fox also knew their lives were on the line. They would take no chances but the chances they had to take.

Angelo Coppi, *Orcus*'s executive officer, had the con. It was beginning to seem they would never find the Russian submarine. Coppi looked wearily at the sonar man.

"Anything?"

"Just background."

Coppi nodded.

"To think I was hoping to bag this turkey for a Christmas present."

Hansen walked into the control room. "What did you expect to do with him? Hang him on the tree?"

Coppi smiled.

"We aren't getting lucky, Skipper."

"Patience, Angel, patience. We may get lucky yet. First contact is a lucky man's game."

"That's for sure."

"I'll take the con. Helm, let's start down to three five zero, okay?"

"Three five zero, sir."

Coppi looked over the sonar man's shoulder as they descended.

"Skipper, it looks like there may be a temperature inversion down here."

"Give me the numbers."

The sonar man hit a switch and his display appeared on the tac/nav display. Hansen looked at it for half a second.

"Good. Looks good. Take her down easy."

Hansen watched the temperature readout.

"There it is. One degree rise. Two. Helm, just skim us into this and then plane up. Hold ballast levels."

"Aye, aye, sir."

The sonar man called out.

"Contact. Middle distant."

"Helm! Take her up fifty."

Hansen smiled.

"Got him."

Brought up quickly by her diving planes, *Orcus* retreated above the inversion. The Russian and American subs were acoustically isolated from one another by a thermal shift that refracted their sounds, making them invisible to one another. Those sounds were faint, for they were a submarine's only real vulnerability and the designers sought diligently to minimize them. On the whole, they succeeded.

Orcus had captured the Russian submarine on her sonar tapes. Now they would turn to the analysis, begin the hunt in earnest.

Orcus was a patient hunter.

D'Alembert had just finished talking with one of his sonar men. It had been hard. D'Alembert didn't find it easy to tell a twenty-three-year-old he might never see home again—for some rather bizarre reasons.

In some ways, fortunately, the junior officers and control room crew were easier to deal with. They knew that the senior officers had effectively made their decision for them. The choice, in consequence, was less of a choice—was less difficult. D'Alembert felt that, in this matter, something resembling a choice, however, was important. Orders were, for once, inappropriate.

They were very nearly past the first point. Soon the third missile would be retargeted on the North Slope. Then would come the arming of the missiles. Then the ultimatum to the Joint Chiefs. Then . . .

Mann woke to the persistence of the alarm clock, switched it off. He rubbed his eyes in the darkness, unwilling to switch on a light. He made his way quietly to the dressing room.

There would be no time for his morning run this morning. The driver was waiting. Mann read the papers as they drove to the Pentagon.

It was now the morning of the last day. That night, Washington time, *Adresteia* was to go "mad," launch on the ASATs. This would be the last full meeting

67

before that scheduled madness, and the last chance to sew up the details of how the affair would be presented to the President after *Adresteia* launched. That was essentially Auslander's chore.

He had better be ready.

Adresteia continued to move with all possible speed, making well in excess of forty knots. They were now far from their expected course, impossible to locate in the vastness of the Pacific. The range of their missiles, which extended to cover an entire hemisphere, was more than adequate for their need. They could reach out far enough if it came to that.

D'Alembert hoped it would not come to that. He did not expect that it would. But if it did . . . he had decided from the first not to hesitate. The Joint Chiefs must be stopped.

Fox had joined him in the wardroom. They were alone.

"What about Morgan?" Fox asked.

D'Alembert attempted a shrug.

"We're all in this together," he said. "It's better she's at least out of the country with the children."

"Switzerland should be a safe place," Fox offered.

D'Alembert nodded acknowledgment. He did not care to discuss it further.

"Alex?"

"Yes?"

"Bird three is ready."

Again d'Alembert nodded.

"Good," he said finally. "Any problems?"

"None, Skipper."

"None?"

"No," Fox said simply. "We're ready for whatever comes next."

"What comes next, Charles, is the arming of the ship's weapons systems. The turning over of the keys. The opening of Pandora's box."

Fox drained his cup, set it down. Waited a moment more.

"Now, Alex?"

"Now. Call Stewart and Thomson to the control room."

Fox went to the ship's intercom and summoned the two necessary officers to join them. He then stood beside the ladder that led to the control room above.

With a single motion d'Alembert stepped past Fox and headed up the ladder.

"Let's do it."

CHAPTER 6

It threatened rain that day as Morgan d'Alembert made her way through the streets of Zurich, walking the short distance from her hotel to the bank she had selected. It was colder than she had anticipated and she regretted wearing nothing warmer than a sweater. She took the steps two at a time, shivering.

"I have an appointment."

"Certainly. Name, please?"

"D'Alembert."

"One moment please, Mrs. d'Alembert."

Thank God bankers spoke English. Her college German would be little help.

She was admitted to the man's office. Meier was a younger man than she expected. She took his hand.

"Herr Meier, I would like to open an account. A numbered account."

Meier weighed the woman for a moment.

"In what amount would you like to open the account, Mrs. d'Alembert?"

She tried her best to appear at ease in this sort of situation.

"Let's say twenty thousand initially. I'll want to arrange for the deposit of several million within a week or two."

Meier opened a desk drawer and removed a sheet of paper. He began to write, speaking while he wrote.

"The confidentiality of your transactions is of particular importance?"

"Yes."

"A 'numbered' account is not strictly necessary for confidentiality, Mrs. d'Alembert. Swiss banking laws assure the absolute privacy of all account transactions. So long as no Swiss laws are broken, of course."

"I see. Mr. Meier, I would still prefer that the account be numbered."

Meier looked up, smiled.

"As you wish."

It was winter. The North Pole was in darkness. The cold pressed hard upon the forms of ice and snow. Nothing moved but the wind.

Orcus hunted beneath the ice. The core of her reactor glowed with the illumination of some secret light. An illumination no man could see and still live. The single propeller turned steadily, silently, driving her on.

It was a warm winter's day in Washington. The morning light reached into the room through the eastward-facing windows. It was the twenty-fourth of December.

Auslander listened closely while the three generals analyzed the detailed arrangements for the destroyer that was to eliminate *Adresteia* shortly after she launched. They were thorough but confident. Auslander, distracted for a moment, wondered idly how the Marine Corps commandant would feel about his exclusion from this summary bit of summitry.

"The timing will be absolutely precise, then."

71

"As long as d'Alembert is on time in his launching."

"He'll be on time."

Auslander studied the momentarily indistinguishable three of them, the complement of close aides. They had finished with d'Alembert.

He decided to speak up.

"Is this element absolutely necessary?" he asked.

"What?" Collier said.

"D'Alembert."

"We've been through this," Shaw said, as much to his colleagues as to Auslander.

"Then let's go through it again, Admiral. *Why* do we have to destroy *Adresteia*?"

Shaw answered him more than a little sharply. "Because, Mr. Secretary, that is our path of least risk. We are running enough risk as it is."

Collier was extremely aggravated. "God damn it, I am *not* going to go through this again. We have other things to worry about. This isn't some fucking morality play, Auslander, whether you like it or not."

Mann intervened quickly.

"Just one second, all right?"

He gave Auslander a placatory look.

"None of us is entirely at ease with this situation. I think we all understand that we have no choice. Mr. Secretary, we all have the deepest respect for you, but I think the simple fact is that we all hate this thing every bit as much as you do. So we're all a little sensitive on the subject," he said, looking in Collier's direction. "But at this point I think the way some of us are handling it is by gritting our teeth and hanging on. We have to."

Mann let this last thought hang in the air. After a

moment or two, General Collier extended his hand across the table. Auslander accepted it.

"The next item," Mann resumed, "is the sequencing of the events immediately following _Adresteia's_ launch. Shall we take it from that point?"

It had begun to rain when Morgan d'Alembert left the bank on Bahnhofstrasse. She stopped to open her umbrella. If she wasn't dressed for the chill wind, at least she was protected from the rain.

Meier had seemed ever so slightly amused by her financial ignorance, she thought, but he had patiently explained the necessary steps for the transfer of money into the account and had volunteered that later investments or disbursements could be carried out in the bank's name. Which helped.

It had gone, in fact, better than she had expected— far better than she had feared. Yet her fears remained. She tried not to think of her husband, of _Adresteia_ somewhere deep beneath the Pacific, but so coldly calculated a confinement of reality was impossible. Emotions had their own reality and were not to be denied. There was, in point of fact, no way for her not to recall their last night together, their final embrace—and to wonder if she would ever see Alex alive again.

She moved alone in a sea of ignorance, utterly isolated. She could not even know if his officers had chosen to support him. Could not know when he would transmit the ultimatum. What the response would be. She could only wait, doing what she could by her presence in Zurich, but largely helpless to act.

She assumed her movements might be watched. If it were to go very suddenly very wrong, she would probably know soon enough.

Yet if Alex succeeded, if the Joint Chiefs chose to concede, there would doubtless be long days of waiting still. Her isolation would continue. Her doubts would continue. Her memories, her fears, would continue.

Her hope, then, depended on the prolongation of her isolation, the extension of her fears. She must steel herself.

She turned her steps down the rain-slick street toward her hotel.

Mann talked for nearly an hour. He was interrupted frequently by questions from Shaw, Collier, occasionally Auslander. Questions that invariably served to further illustrate the extent of Mann's anticipated orchestrations. Mann was on top of it.

Finally, he began to assemble his notes neatly before him on the table, reducing the separate neat piles to a single neat pile.

"Any further questions?"

There were none.

"Then we go with it as written."

There were no dissensions. A measure of expectation devolved upon Auslander. He lit his pipe, cleared his throat.

"The President will encounter no difficulties in the cover scenario as written—it will carry him. I'll phone him around noon on the 'discovery' of the ASATs. No problem."

Somewhat hesitantly, Shaw spoke.

"You're confident of that, Mr. Secretary?"

"Absolutely. You know your tactics. I know my President."

"Then we're ready," Collier said, rising from the table.

Shaw, too, rose. "We're counting on you, Mr. Secretary. You understand that."

Auslander puffed on his pipe. "You can count on me, gentlemen."

Mann stood, looked down at him.

"We are."

Orcus considered its prey.

The submarine's computers could do a great deal in analyzing sound patterns, sifting the ocean for a submarine. Still, the sonar operator was the key.

Orcus's sonar man replayed the tape another time.

"No question, Skipper. Distant, running quiet—my guess eight or nine knots. He's in a sound channel, but I'd guess his heading is near ours. Range is impossible to say. Thirty-plus."

"Any chance he heard us?"

The sonar man weighed the factors. Shook his head definitively.

"No, Skipper. He was barely within my threshold values. We were outside his for sure."

"Good. That'll make it that much simpler."

Hansen turned to his executive officer. "She's yours, Angel. Start shadowing him."

"Helm, give me one nine five at fourteen knots," Coppi said.

"Aye, aye, sir, one nine five at fourteen."

Hansen turned to leave the control room.

"I'm exhausted, Angel. Wake me in five hours. Sooner if you have to. Okay?"

"Okay, Skipper."

Coppi turned to the beginning of the chase.

* * *

For the few intervening hours Auslander did little but plan the brief call he would place at noon. It had to be right. Precisely right.

At noon he told his secretary to place the call. He waited.

"The President will talk to you now, Mr. Secretary."

The next voice on the line was Spencer Elliott's.

"Merry Christmas, Bill. What can I do for you?"

"I've got some pretty bad news, Mr. President."

"What?"

"It seems the Soviets have deployed a significant ASAT capability concealed in three sites we thought were only capable of shaking up the Chinese a bit."

Auslander could almost hear Elliott's mind closing in on the problem.

"How bad, Bill?"

"If the analyses are on the money they can take out nearly three-quarters of our strategic C^3."

"Operational?"

"Looks like."

"They know we know?"

"Stealth went in clean."

"What does Mann say?"

Auslander looked out the window.

"Mann's been stewing with this for a couple of days, Mr. President."

"How the hell is that?" Elliott demanded.

"Well, the Joint Chiefs and the CIA have been trying pretty desperately to develop their own options—especially the Joint Chiefs."

Elliott sighed in disgust.

"Do they have any?"

"No. Not yet. Mann had Shaw give a Trident captain retargeting coordinates and gave him first priority in a shooting war. They briefed the guy in full before they even came to me. I think they're running scared on this thing."

"I can see that."

Auslander cleared his throat. "Listen, Mr. President, this isn't my idea of the ideal holiday, but I thought you should know what was in the wind down here."

"I appreciate that, Bill."

"I promised them I'd sit on this for a day or two, Mr. President, longer if it was necessary—so I'd appreciate your discretion on this."

"Sure, sure. Are those clowns keeping close tabs on this thing?"

"The whole problem, as they see it, is that we can't tell with confidence if they're up to anything imminent. And we can't do anything about it if they are. It's a serious threat."

"I know."

Elliott seemed to be taking a moment to think about it.

"Okay, Bill, keep your ear to the ground. I don't want anything too hasty on this. I suspect we're going to have to come down pretty hard on the Soviets on this one. I don't like the feel of it."

"Neither do I, Mr. President."

With that they rang off. Auslander deposited the receiver on its cradle, walked slowly over to the window. Stared blindly into the falling rain.

D'Alembert took the con. The officers were in the control room with him, occupying the available space with their solemnity.

There were several alternate means of arming the missiles. The swiftest way, the standard procedure, was routed through the centralized computers which monitored the ship's performance and position, updated the missiles' guidance system.

Thomson, as weapons officer, took the small console at the side of the room. The console was virtually identical with the other terminals spaced through the critical control areas of the ship. Thomson would enter the words, which would then be displayed on his screen as well as on the tac/nav display for all to see.

D'Alembert stood, flanked by the exec and the engineering officer. Unconsciously, all three men stood with arms folded.

It was time.

D'Alembert spoke softly.

"System."

Thomson typed in the word, which appeared instantly on the display—followed by the computers' response.

—READY.

"Call Supervisor."

—SUPERVISOR READY.

"Arm Sequence."

—ARM SEQ READY. VERIFY.

"Systems Arm."

—SYS ARM. TEST?

"No test."

—VERIFIED. SYS UP.

—WARNING: NO COMMAND DECISION MONITORED.

"Op-Code 1."

—READY. WEAPONS OFFICER INDENT.

Thomson silently typed in his key number.

"9AB1 (X) ."

—VERIFIED. ENGINEERING OFFICER IDENT.

Stewart seemed to address the computers directly as he intoned his key.

"01D6 (X) ."

—VERIFIED. EXECUTIVE OFFICER IDENT.

"73EC (X) ."

—VERIFIED. COMMANDER IDENT.

"AB3A (X) ."

—VERIFIED. FURNISH ALPHA AUTHENTICATORS IN SEQUENCE.

Thomson entered his word.

"Colorlessness."

The others followed quickly.

"Evening."

"Ready."

"Shadow."

—VERIFIED. READY.

D'Alembert dictated swiftly to Thomson now. His officers had verified to the computers' satisfaction that this was an authorized act of war. The system was now his.

"Status Word Access. Mask 1011."

—VERIFIED SW MASK.

"Access Core Address 000A (X) . System Memory Mask 0011."

—READY.

D'Alembert was about to reach into the computers' programming and shift the program in such a way that the ship's missiles and torpedoes would not be fully armed but would instead be armed immediately on his providing a key word of his own.

"Load Memory AB3A (X) ."

—READY.

"Execute."

The computers worked collectively for a few nano-seconds.

—ARMED.

—WAITING.

—COUNTER RUNNING.

D'Alembert spoke quickly.

"System Stand By."

—COUNTER?

"No Counter. Mask 0."

—COUNTER OPEN.

—STANDING BY.

Now to seal the shifted program.

"System."

—READY.

"Execute."

—DONE.

The display went suddenly blank, replaced by the standard tac/nav display.

The ship's officers looked at one another soberly. *Adresteia* was now on a very quick reaction basis. The moment d'Alembert provided the computers with his key word all systems would be fully armed and ready to launch ballistic missiles, antisubmarine rockets, or torpedoes. They had ceded to him that final authority.

Adresteia was ready.

CHAPTER 7

Elliott had no meetings scheduled for that day. The helicopter, in fact, was scheduled to fly him to Camp David in less than an hour—to spend the holiday there with his family. He wondered, momentarily, if he should postpone or cancel the flight.

He thought better of it. He was every bit as close to the telephone in Camp David as he was in the White House. For better or worse. It would make no difference. Auslander did not seem to expect anything immediate, and he needed the rest, the shift in perspective. He needed, too, under the circumstances, to appear as if everything were well in hand.

He told his secretary, then, to phone the Secretary of State, Edwin I. Moore. It took her fifteen minutes to track him down. When she did. Elliott informed him of Auslander's warning, of the ASATs. Moore was duly alarmed.

"Mr. President, I see two areas of significant confrontation stemming from this development. Both are, in my estimation, equally perilous. Firstly, we are thrust into a situation of tactical confrontation with the Soviets over this matter. It puts us in an extraordinarily delicate position with respect to our negotiating posture. Secondly, I suspect that your administration will find itself in an equally hazardous dilemma with respect to the military."

That then, succinctly put, precisely inflected, was the judgment of the Secretary of State.

Elliott then informed Moore that, according to Auslander, General Mann had already taken first precautionary steps, giving special instructions to a missile submarine commander in event of precipitate action on the part of the Soviets and that, evidently, the Joint Chiefs were thus far at a loss for acceptable options.

Moore weighed these facts.

"I find this situation distressing, Mr. President."

"So do I."

"It suggests a formidable level of determination on the part of the Pentagon—and, by extension, the liaison wing of CIA."

"Agreed. Not that such a reaction is exactly astonishing, considering the nature of the threat."

"Well, I suppose I see some truth in that, Mr. President, but, still, I am no partisan of General Mann's— or his drinking buddies."

Elliott considered this last assessment before asking if the Secretary of State had any specific recommendations.

He did not. "For the moment, Mr. President, I'd like to think this over further. I would feel strongly, however, that, if I were in your position, I would not give the Joint Chiefs an eternity to come around to me with their revelations."

"I'll probably give them several days—maybe a week. Those sites have been in operation, apparently, for a while at least—according to Auslander. I don't think a few days, realistically, is going to make much of a difference."

"You'd rather see how they approach the matter without tipping your hand?"

"Yes."

With that, their conversation quickly concluded itself. It was time for the helicopter. Elliott looked quickly around the office, making certain he hadn't overlooked anything.

He picked up the briefcase. It was heavy. He had added material on ASATs to the weight of it. He had homework to do, holiday or no. The Joint Chiefs would wait, but they wouldn't wait forever, and Elliott would be ready for them.

He closed the door behind himself and headed for the helipad.

Coppi held the con for several hours as *Orcus* stalked the unknown Russian submarine. Periodically they deployed their towed array sonar but, primarily, they relied on their bow sonar. A good deal of this sort of work was inspired guesswork and skill rather than hard science.

Hansen entered the control room, surveyed the tac/nav display, pondered the sonar man's most recent data.

"Okay, Angel," he announced. "I'll take her for a while."

"All yours, Skipper."

Coppi was glad for the break.

"Nice job, Angel."

"We should be closing in a few more hours—with luck."

Hansen nodded.

"Then the fun begins."

General Mann was "off" now, officially enjoying the holiday. He met his youngest son, Martin, at the air base, watching as the young man's fighter touched down, taxied slowly toward the ramp.

"Any trouble getting permission to fly here?" the father asked.

"Not really. I needed the flight time."

Mann nodded. They drove in silence through the Virginia suburbs.

"What's your time-in-type now?"

Making conversation.

"Two thirty."

"Getting there."

"I guess so."

"Do you like the F-16?"

"Yeah. I do. Of course, I haven't had much to compare with it. The weight's nice, worth the tradeoff in payload, I think. The turning acceleration is incredible."

Mann nodded. He looked at his watch.

"Anything wrong, Dad? You seem distracted."

Martin was his favorite.

"No. Nothing. Don't want to keep your mother waiting."

"Oh."

"That's all. Nothing special."

Stewart had the con, Michaels keeping him company in the control room. The two were essentially engaged in passing the remaining hours till *Adresteia* was to transmit d'Alembert's ultimatum to the Joint Chiefs.

"What do you think of the North Slope aspect?" Michaels asked the older man.

"I don't know, not much to say about it, really. I can't think of a lesser threat that would expose them— be taken seriously."

Michaels opted for a try at black comedy.

"We could blow up the Pentagon."

Stewart wasn't entirely amused.

"Right."

There was a minor awkward silence between the two men. Finally, Michaels said, "It just seems so . . . strange . . . *bizarre*—you know what I mean?"

Stewart answered noncommittally.

"I know."

Auslander, too, was waiting. Doing other things. He did his best to appear at his ease over dinner. It seemed to go well enough, and any signs of what might, in retrospect, be thought to have been signs of nervousness would seem natural enough, considering the phone call he had made to Elliott that afternoon. Natural to be a little on edge.

He found himself looking at the time too often, tried to stifle the unthinking impulse. Certainly he knew what time it was, minute to minute, without needing to consult the clock. It was more a matter of bringing reassurance to his consciousness that time was, in the unconscious world, still passing.

So the time passed.

Collier, too, passed the time in normalcy, in the expected events of a holiday evening, family, friends. The word would first come late that night, relayed through Mann. D'Alembert, "mad" though he was, would not launch his missiles without forewarning his countrymen, alerting them to any Soviet reaction. That unexpected warning would come precisely ten minutes before launch.

Launch, in turn, would come at midnight, Washington time. *Adresteia*, of course, kept to her own time, Greenwich Mean Time. For *Adresteia* the clock would read 0500 GMT.

In the Pacific, in fact, it would be another time entirely. Another day.

Shaw glanced at his watch. Seven thirty-five.

"Pass the salt, please."

Orcus narrowed the gap steadily, skirting the temperature inversion while it lasted, taking advantage of its separation to close the distance more swiftly than would otherwise be possible. Then the inversion shifted, became useless, forcing *Orcus* to reduce speed, at this close range, to twelve knots. She made that speed now, assured of running more silently than her prey.

The engineering officer relieved Hansen, taking up the slow chase for several hours, further closing the distance.

He spoke into the intercom.

"Captain Hansen, Mr. Coppi, to the control room, please."

When the two men arrived they were informed that they were now thought to be within three miles of the Russian submarine.

"Good work," Hansen said.

"Is he still running steady?" Coppi asked.

"A jink here and there, but that's about it," the engineering officer reported.

"Doesn't say an awful lot for him, does it?" Hansen asked them rhetorically.

There was no need for an answer.

"Changing course, Skipper," the current sonar man called out.

"Dead stop, gentlemen."

Hansen waited.

"Coming about to port, Skipper. Turning easy. Maybe coming up a bit."

"Very well, give me dead slow and come to one eight zero for a bit."

The order was quickly executed. Hansen noted the new course of the enemy submarine.

"Okay, helm, make that one nine five now and let's try ahead one-third. Hold her level. Let's see if we can't get in a little closer before we tag him."

Inexorably, *Orcus* closed upon the Russian.

General Mann's part in the closely scheduled charade began precisely at ten fifty that evening when his chief aide, on duty at the Pentagon, phoned him. The telephone lines were secure, but the conversation stuck to the script for security's sake.

"Sorry to disturb you, General, but we may have a problem here."

"Go ahead."

"Sir, I would have gone to Admiral Shaw with this ordinarily, but I felt you should be advised that we have a submarine significantly overdue on a routine check-in—*Adresteia*, sir."

There was no hesitation on Mann's end of the line. "I'll be right in."

Mann made his hasty excuses, as planned, drove, as planned, directly to the Pentagon. There, in position to move quickly on word of *Adresteia*'s launching against the ASATs, he awaited the final message.

Eternally restless, *Adresteia* moved swiftly through the darkness of the Pacific.

Twenty-three thousand two hundred miles above the Pacific, NavSynch 7 stood stationary, rotating with the earth in geosynchronous orbit, waiting.

D'Alembert took the con.

"Bleed ballast. Helm, three degrees up bubble. Sound by the hundred."

"Aye, aye, Captain. Three up, by the hundred."

Adresteia began the long climb toward the surface. The transmission was ready, held in the bubble memory of a computer. Their laser carrier beam would instruct NavSynch 7 to relay the encrypted message to General Mann through the computerized command network. They rose quickly.

"One hundred meters."

"Two degrees down bubble. Call off by tens."

They slowly neared the surface.

"Dead slow. Bring her to periscope depth."

D'Alembert waited. He watched the display of data projected on the tac/nav display.

"Periscope depth, Captain."

"Array one, up."

Array one was a sensor probe.

"One is up, Captain."

Fox stood beside the operator.

"Clear, Skipper."

"Two up."

The motors whirred again, bringing the communications array above the waves.

"Two up."

"Communications, tie in to seven."

The ship's inertial navigation system knew their position within meters. The computers also knew Nav-Synch 7's position with comparable accuracy. They directed the tight laser beam to the orbiting satellite.

"Locked on."

"Transmit."

The message was passed in a single coded microsecond burst of invisible light.

"Acknowledged, Captain."

D'Alembert looked at Fox.

"Take us down, gentlemen."

As simply as that, it was done.

As Mann slowly paced, waiting, the message was relayed by NavSynch 7 through the various electronic links to the military command center where computers passed it, in turn, still secure in its computer-generated code, to the decoding center nearest Mann's office. Within seconds of its transmission the priority message was in the hands of the waiting aide.

The aide entered briskly, without knocking, crossed the room quickly. Handed the message to Mann. There was such a quality of haste in the man's step that Mann knew, even before he had seen the message, that something had gone very, very wrong.

The message, illumined in the sharp cone of light of the tensor, read:

—SIR;

—ADRESTEIA WILL NOT CARRY OUT HER AS-
SIGNED TASK. NOR WILL ANY OTHER VESSEL.

—WE ARE PRESENTLY TARGETED THREE MISSILES
ON NORTH SLOPE ALASKA PRODUCTION SITES.

—YOU WILL:

—1) ABANDON FIRST STRIKE.

—2) PREPARE FOR THE EXPEDITIOUS TRANSFER
TWENTY-FIVE MILLION US CURRENCY TO A SWISS AC-
COUNT TO BE DESIGNATED.

—BE AWARE THAT I AM OF THE UNDERSTAND-
ING THAT OUR ORDERS WERE NOT I REPEAT NOT AU-
THORIZED BY THE COMMANDER IN CHIEF.

—I WILL REESTABLISH CONTACT IN THREE
HOURS.

—YOU WILL TAKE NO ACTION AGAINST THIS VES-
SEL, HER PERSONNEL, OR THEIR KIN.

—YOU WILL ABANDON THIS MISSION. OR I
LAUNCH.

                                    D'ALEMBERT

Mann was, for once, taken completely off his guard.
He looked for a while at the aide, then again at the
message, its wording. Finally, he laughed. It was a difficult laugh to characterize.

Mann read the ultimatum through one more time,
smiling grimly to himself. Then he folded the piece of
paper carefully, put it in his coat pocket. Removed his
reading glasses. Looked at the wall display that
mapped the intended ASATs. Switched it off.

"Charlie, I think we have a problem."

The aide nodded.

The general sighed. It was the one moment of

doubt, of indecision, the aide had ever seen him evidence. It would be the last.

"Ring up Collier and our stalwart friend the Secretary of Defense and tell them the news."

"Yes, sir. Anything else, sir?"

"Not for the moment. I want to call Shaw myself."

The aide left Mann to the problem at hand.

Shaw answered the phone on the first ring. He immediately recognized Mann's voice.

"Who is the best sub killer in the U.S. Navy?"

CHAPTER 8

Quenten Essex Devlin, Deputy Chief of Naval Operations for Submarine Warfare, was the best sub killer in the United States Navy.

Devlin knew it. Admiral David T. Shaw, CNO, knew it, too. Thus it was that late that night Devlin was drawn to what suddenly threatened to become a nightmare for the Joint Chiefs—and for others as well.

Devlin had been sleeping soundly. His wife of nearly twenty years, Maureen, had died a little over a year ago, succumbing with cruel suddenness to cancer. Devlin had loved her. He had only recently begun to evolve beyond the sense of shock and loss. Those feelings were, he knew, inevitable. Natural. To be expected. Which changed things not at all.

He had chosen to spend the evening alone. To turn in early. He had finally managed a sound sleep when the ringing of the telephone drew him reluctantly back to the world of the living.

"Hello?" he managed.

Devlin, sleepy though he was, immediately recognized the urgent—almost frantic—voice on the other end of the line as being that of the Chief of Naval Operations.

"Christ, Devlin, are you asleep?"

"Not any more."

"Well, get your ass in here, Devlin. I need you. Fast."

"What's up?"

"*Adresteia*'s gone renegade."

Devlin was no longer asleep.

Orcus had continued carefully to close on the Soviet submarine. Hansen continued the delicate task, narrowing the distance with the hours until he felt they were near enough to take the Russina by surprise.

"Sonar?"

The sonar man on duty consulted with his instruments again. "Probably less than two miles, Skipper."

"Angel?"

"I think we should go for him."

Hansen nodded agreement with his executive officer.

"Wait a minute, Skipper," the sonar man interrupted them. "I think he's maneuvering again. May be heading up."

"What's the overhead?"

"Thin ice, Skipper. Less than a meter."

"He's going up to call home," Coppi observed.

"We may as well do likewise," Hansen said. "First, however . . ."

Hansen spoke briskly.

"Angel, sound battle stations. Diving officer, begin slow ballasting for surface. Helm, hold her level by the planes." Hansen quickly considered the tactical display. "Okay, give me two-thirds ahead. Let's wake him up."

Orcus began to accelerate. Hansen studying the numbers as their speed built, their ballast grew steadily lighter. He gave new orders to the diving officer.

They were held submerged now only by the effort of the diving planes and their forward speed. A precise balance.

Thirty knots. *Orcus* wanted up.

"Helm, come to one eight seven."

Thirty-five knots.

"Sonar, you awake?"

"Yes, sir."

"Glad to hear it."

Thirty-seven knots. Bearing down fast.

Hansen could well imagine the Russian captain's face when he learned of *Orcus* bursting on him out of nowhere, flying for him at speed. It would ruin his day.

Sonar called out. "He's detected us, Skipper. Accelerating."

"Helm, take her up. Give him berth to starboard. Sonar, switch to active ranging."

Orcus began to sound actively now, emitting high-energy sound pulses.

They started up.

"Sonar, finger him with the laser."

The precision range-finding beam found him. Data appeared on *Orcus*'s display.

"He's sending a message, Skipper."

"Read it."

" 'Touché.' "

Hansen, pleased, smiled. "Acknowledge. Reply: 'Care to join us for tea?' "

They were still closing swiftly.

"Engineering, reduce speed to one-third. Helm, take her up. Easy does it."

With that the game went to *Orcus*.

* * *

Having rushed to the Pentagon with all possible speed, unshaven and hastily dressed, Devlin was immediately confronted with the fact of waiting. Shaw emerged briefly from Mann's office to tell Devlin it would be a while until he was needed. He was told only that *Adresteia* had gone renegade and that he was to consider how she might be stopped. Nothing further for the moment.

Amazed by his late-night summons, even more so by the brief explanation, Devlin attempted to cozen the time by pondering the meaning of all this. Why in hell would *Adresteia*—d'Alembert—go renegade? What did "renegade" really *mean*? He surely didn't know.

Evidently they would be a good while before they were ready for him, so Devlin left the company of the two armed guards posted beside the door for a cafeteria where he secured himself a tepid cup of black coffee from a vending machine. Then to his situation room where he reconsidered the deployment of all submarines operating in the Pacific. He asked the two men and the one woman on duty there a few questions, but they seemed to know of nothing unusual. *Adresteia*'s position was not precisely known. That, in itself, was not unusual. The situation room knew where *Adresteia* was supposed to be, but they had had no recent position report—so they did not actually know where she was. She could be anywhere. It was a big ocean.

D'Alembert had served under him on the *Benjamin Franklin*. He was a protégé. What would prompt d'Alembert, of all people . . . ?

Devlin quickly put a hold on this line of personal internal inquiry. He was wasting his time. He knew nothing. Yet. He would have to wait on the men closeted in Mann's office.

He would try and consider the worst case. If he had to track down and destroy *Adresteia*, could he do it?

He waited, pacing steadily before the guarded door.

The vessel that was the subject and object of Devlin's speculations, and the Joint Chiefs' and Defense Secretary's more specific quandary, *Adresteia*, had descended to her normal operating depths and resumed her cautious course. Her immediate problem was to wait out the next three hours. It would be a time of slow passage.

D'Alembert did not think the span of time allotted would seem so generous to Mann and the others. What few doubts he had would finally be settled when he ordered contact reestablished. If he were in any way wrong in his suppositions, it would then become clear. If, in the more likely alternative, he was right, that, too, would become clear.

He glanced offhandedly at the ship's chronometer. "Anyone for a game of chess?"

The meeting was conducted in General Mann's office rather than that of the Secretary of Defense because he—not Auslander—had summoned them. It was a dark night for the four men in that room. Not so much a meeting, at first, but a small war.

Auslander was the most resentful and the most hostile. He had been drinking. Collier and Shaw were, for their part, infuriated by what they perceived as Auslander's cowardice.

Mann watched as they directed their own fear and anger toward Auslander. He held himself as nearly aloof as possible, letting the bitterness turn against itself, ground itself. He hoped the inchoate patterns of fear and loathing that filled the room would clarify themselves. Or at least pause for a breath of air.

If they were going to accomplish anything, if he was going to save their collective hides—and he was—they had to move fast. They didn't have all night. They had less than two hours.

Mann raised his voice, suddenly, filling the large room.

"Enough!"

It was indeed enough. Mann had a voice that could raise the dead or slay the living.

"Enough," he said in a more resigned tone of voice. "I want to know one thing and one thing only: What are we going to do?"

Shaw, Collier, Auslander, slowly found their way to their seats. Auslander then thought better of it, stood.

"General Mann," he said, "I don't seem to recall asking you to chair this meeting."

"You didn't," Mann said, unable for a moment to conceal his contempt. "Do you have any suggestions?"

"Damn it, Mann, I am not going to put up with this . . . crap. Now you listen to me and listen to me well, General. I am your superior."

This last seemed a particulary doubtful statement in any of a number of ways and Mann could only shake his head.

"Then you tell me what to do, Mr. Secretary."

This sudden acquiescence, ironic as it was, seemed to throw Auslander completely off his guard. "Well . . . under the circumstances . . . there's nothing we can do. We'll call it off. We can work out a transfer of the money somehow. We'll have to concede to him."

"Concede?" Collier asked incredulously. "Concede? Are you out of your mind, Auslander? Concede to what? Blackmail?"

Auslander slowly took his seat, relished its support. "General, I don't care what you want to call it and I don't care what you think of it. D'Alembert has stopped us dead in our tracks."

Shaw spoke next.

"He has a point, whether we like it or not. D'Alembert has stopped us cold. Acceding to his demands may be the only way out. Or else we might get to the point where he has no choice but to actually launch. That would expose us utterly. We wouldn't survive." Shaw toyed with his pen for a moment. "He's got us by the short hairs."

Auslander, perceiving an advantage, pressed on. "Look, we're stuck in this situation. I don't want to try and assess blame at this point. . . ." He looked toward Mann, then extended his gaze to the other two men. "We've all been at fault or in error—or just plain had bad luck with d'Alembert—how could he manage this, anyway? How could he get his officers behind him? Maybe they're not?"

"Inconceivable," Shaw said.

"Agreed," Collier said.

"He wouldn't have gotten to the point of sending that message," Mann explained for the secretary, "if he didn't have his crew behind him."

"Perhaps we could fragment them?" Auslander speculated. "If we could create dissension . . ."

"How do you propose to do that?" Mann asked pointedly.

"Well, when we talk to them I'm sure that a certain

number of his officers will be involved in the conversation, listening in . . ." Auslander floundered visibly. "No, that wouldn't work."

"He controls that boat," Shaw said. "Believe it, Mr. Secretary. Believe it. You can't sneak behind his back like a bureaucrat and undercut him."

Auslander hesitated.

"Then that proves my point. There's nothing to do under these circumstances but give in. Buy him off. Keep him quiet. Jesus, I just spoke to Elliott this afternoon. If he ever finds out what we've been up to . . ."

Auslander's outburst was met by silence.

"We have to do *something*," he said.

Mann had had enough. If there were more time he might have let the bedlam continue. They had very little time. D'Alembert would be reestablishing contact. They had to be ready for him.

"Mr. Secretary," he began, "this has thrown us all way off balance. Put us on the defensive. We have to regain that balance. We have to recapture the offensive. We have to see *Adresteia* stopped and we have to see those ASATs put out of commission—if we can still find a way. We also have to stall the President as long as possible in order to have the time we need to do these things."

The three men listened.

"Mr. Secretary, I would ask you to trust us to be able to handle d'Alembert. What we need you to do is to handle the President. Buy us the time we need."

Mann looked at Auslander. Auslander nodded a feeble acknowledgement. Tentative. He would listen. He wanted a way out.

Mann turned then to General Collier.

"Mike, I want you to oversee our security. I want you to ride herd on everything except the President—CIA, NSA, our own people. That's critical."

"No problem."

"Good. Dave, I need you to find a way of taking out *Adresteia* clean. That's supposed to be impossible."

"Yes. It is."

"I want to try, Dave."

The CNO considered carefully. He could make no promises.

"I'll try."

"Good. I, for my part, will try and develop an alternate strategy for the ASATs. I don't think it's going to be possible, under these circumstances, but I intend to give it one hell of a try."

Mann drummed his fingers on the table.

"Mr. Secretary, do you have any objection to my leading this strategy session?" he asked in his most diplomatic voice.

"No. I'll reserve judgment."

"Fair enough. My first priority is how to handle d'Alembert when he links with the command net and what the possibilities are of being able to handle him at sea."

There was agreement that this was the first problem to be tackled.

"Dave, what are our chances?"

Morgan d'Alembert looked out her window and down upon the night-lit streets of Zurich. The children, Joshua and Jennifer, were asleep at long last, and she was alone with her thoughts. Again.

She left the window, sat down on the edge of the bed, tried leafing through some magazines, attempting a measure of interest. Failed. She tried the book she had picked up at the airport, again attempting interest. Again failing. Finally, she switched on the television set. It made, of course, no difference whatsoever. She turned it off. Walked slowly back to the window. Looked out at the lights that determined the shape of the darkness.

She should know how to wait by now, she told herself; she had waited long enough while Alex was away on the long patrols. But she knew better. This was different. Far different. It was as if he had gone to war. In a way, she knew, he had. He might not come back.

There had been no stars the night he left. She remembered that. It had been raining—or snowing. She was surprised to realize that she did not remember which. Strange where memory carried you. A scent, a touch, a single image, but seldom the thing whole.

The bank account she could manage. The code word, long awaited, she could manage. She would not fail Alex. Would not fail herself. She told herself these things, once again, and knew them to be true.

She also knew it to be true that she was more uniquely alone, separated from him, than she had ever been, that the character of her loneliness was both far greater and far different than it had ever been before. It was like learning a new texture of pain—seemingly impossible before the fact, but all too clear in the experience itself.

Pain, she knew, could be endured. Alex, too, countless thousands of miles away, commanding *Adresteia*, bore his share of the isolation, the anxiety, the doubt. She would bear hers, too, alone, and their sharing that fearful isolation, each, alone, would somehow join them across the miles.

She remembered the touch of his hand on her bare shoulder for an instant. Placed her own hand on that same spot. Held it there.

She watched the houselights below begin to depart from the night, one by one, yielding the night to the streetlights that defined corridors through the darkness. She did not doubt herself, did not doubt that she would bear the fear and loneliness for as long as it must be borne—but she did doubt, for a time, that morning would ever come to the silent streets below.

Devlin paced the length of the hall, sat for a while, paced some more. He asked one of the guards if he had a piece of gum. The man didn't. Neither did the other.

They always came in pairs, he thought.

He resumed his pacing.

Aboard *Adresteia* Michaels had the con, Stewart at his side. The two men made small talk.

Below, in the wardroom, the captain and the executive officer played at chess.

Fox made a move. D'Alembert studied it.

"Your mind isn't on the game, Charles."

A cold front had moved into Washington in the last few hours. A light snow fell on the Pentagon as three A.M. neared.

Mann looked at his watch.

"Do you think he'll be precisely on time?" Auslander asked.

"Count on it," Shaw said. "We can't home on the laser carrier to NavSynch 7, we don't know his position. . . . He'll be on time."

Collier had just been grilled on how he might maintain their security. They were not being unnecessarily kind to one another that night.

"Mr. Secretary," Collier said, exasperated, "I have *got* to know if you can hold off the President."

"I don't know. I honestly don't know. I think I may be able to. But I need to know what to tell him if this begins to unravel at some point—which it may. We have to decide on that. It's important."

Shaw spoke.

"For a fallback on the President, why don't we essentially tough it out? D'Alembert intends to launch on the Soviets. We're trying to stop him."

"And we've been keeping it from the President?" Mann asked.

"Sure, why not?" Collier put in. "It makes sense. If we try and make ourselves look too good it just looks suspicious. So we admit to trying to cover our tails. If we try and look like virtuous saints it won't hold."

"But," Auslander said, "if we accept looking bad on trying to stop d'Alembert from launching on the ASATs without having to run to the President . . . at least we're credible."

"I like it," Shaw said. "It plays to the right prejudices."

"It rings true," Collier said.

"Okay, I agree," Mann concluded. "Our position, then, is that we gave d'Alembert new target assignments and emphasized the importance of his moving fast in the event of action by the Russians. There was a misunderstanding, a failure of communications at some personal level, and d'Alembert undertook to act on his own. We didn't intend that at all and have been trying desperately to stop him."

Mann considered his summary.

"It will only hold so far," he said. "Just so far and no farther. But I think it's the best we can do for the moment. Stall him, Mr. Secretary, and if you have to lay it out, lay it out that way. It should buy us the time we need. Can you make it fly?"

"I think I can live with it," Auslander answered. "I'll leak it that way if it becomes necessary."

"This angle will help on security, too," Collier said. "The number of people we have who are actually in a position to distinguish between this cover and our real intent is very small—somewhere around fifteen or sixteen I'd guess offhand. I'll have to work out the details, but I'd think we can keep it in that neighborhood."

"And all of us have a personal stake," Mann added. "Gentlemen, I think we're getting a handle on all this."

He turned then to the CNO.

"Dave, I guess it's back to you again."

Shaw cleared his throat. Took a sip of coffee.

"I don't know what to say. *Adresteia* is damn good. D'Alembert is damn good. We have a very real problem. D'Alembert is desperate. Just as with everything else we've touched on so far tonight, there are a number of different ways to go and we don't have time to evaluate them all fully. We have to go on instinct."

"Do you want to call in Devlin?"

"No. I'd rather deal with this initial communication with d'Alembert first," Shaw said. "By my watch we only have ten minutes. I don't want Devlin in on this. He's got to be kept out of the inner circle, held to the same version we intend to feed the President."

"You don't trust him?" Mann asked.

"Not that way, no. He and d'Alembert have been pretty tight. They're both submariners, and I'm not. Devlin can be very strong-headed about some things—he's the best I've got and we need his advice, but we can't risk his finding out the truth about all this. He'll be a fair test of the story we intend to feed Elliott, though, I'll tell you that."

"All right," Mann said. "I respect your judgment on that."

Mann, too, glanced at his watch.

"First d'Alembert," he said. "Then Devlin."

CHAPTER 9

D'Alembert made another move. Fox studied it, looked up from the board.

"That's it, Alex. I concede."

D'Alembert smiled.

"It's time to end the game, anyway."

Fox looked at the chronometer on the bulkhead.

"Or start it."

General Collier was speaking.

"I think we should just draw him out at this point as much as possible—we should play it safe and close to the vest. We don't know exactly where he's coming from at this point, anyway."

"I basically agree with you," Shaw said, "although I think we have a pretty fair idea where he's coming from—but d'Alembert won't stay near the surface chattering away with us. Not for any length of time—it's the one time he's potentially vulnerable."

"Not *very* vulnerable, though," Auslander put in.

"No," Shaw agreed. "His transmissions are on a very tight beam, directed almost vertically. NavSynch replies through a modulator—useless for localizing. Unless you already knew where to look for him, the satellite transmissions are useless. Still, he'll stay deep-submerged and quiet. His undetectability is his greatest asset."

"He'll be free to take *some* time, won't he?" Collier asked.

"Sure. But I think we can count on him to be very careful about it."

Mann's chief aide entered.

"The link you wanted is complete, sir."

"Any problem keeping it secure?"

"No, sir, General Collier. I programmed it through personally."

"Good."

Auslander was the first to rise from his chair. They had agreed that Mann would handle all communications with d'Alembert.

"Maybe this is d'Alembert's idea of a practical joke," Auslander offered.

There were no takers. The four men and the aide entered the communications room attached to Mann's complex of offices.

Closed the door.

"I have the con. Let's take her up, gentlemen."

Minutes later *Adresteia* neared the surface, periscope depth.

"Still clear, sonar?"

"Clear, Captain."

"Hold her at periscope depth, helm."

Adresteia's radar and electronic arrays were extended above the waves, the electronic link extended through the omnipresent NavSynch 7. NavSynch 7, in turn, relayed through a choice of down-links through the command net, where the anticipated communication was shuttled to Mann's communications office by the program his aide had readied. The message was computer-encrypted in what was known as a trapdoor code from the moment of transmission to the moment of final receipt. Thus it was ultimately secure, bound in a computerized web of secrecy.

D'Albert spoke to his communications officer.

"Link-up?"

"Achieved, Captain, but they will only handle alpha material—no voice, sir."

D'Alembert smiled grimly to himself. Fox looked at him.

"They won't risk the possibility of a voice-tape at this point," Fox said meaningfully. D'Alembert nodded.

"Okay, we'll do it their way."

He would speak to them, then, through the communications man. It defined the limits of the conversation.

"Greetings, gentlemen."

The words were typed up quickly, appearing on *Adresteia*'s tac/nav display, followed by the equally swift reply.

"Good morning, Captain. What can we do for you?"

"When will the sum be ready for transfer?" d'Alembert demanded of the men in the Pentagon.

"We are considering that," was the reply.

"You will cancel the mission."

"We are considering that, too."

D'Alembert was angered.

"You had better consider quickly," he said to the operator and the indifferent screen.

"We are doing our best."

"Who am I talking to?"

"Mann."

"Are the others there?"

"What others?"

"Auslander, the Joint Chiefs."

"They are," Mann granted.

D'Alembert considered Mann's recalcitrance.

"Are you or are you not prepared to talk?" he asked them.

"We prefer to consider the matter further."

Mann was determined to tough it out. Considering the circumstances, d'Alembert thought, he was playing the game pretty hard. He turned to Fox. "I don't like this attitude at all."

"I don't think we're supposed to like it," Fox said.

D'Alembert nodded curtly.

"General, you will not engage me in stalling tactics. I am fully prepared to launch."

The delay that followed seemed infinite. The eyes of his officers were on d'Alembert. The reply came.

"We will take no precipitate action, d'Alembert. Do not be unnecessarily hasty."

D'Alembert took his temper and held it firmly in check. He moved on.

"Will you guarantee the safety of my crew at this time?"

"Yes."

So far so good.

"My requirements?"

"We will consider your demands, Captain," the screen said. "We need time."

"How much time?"

"Twelve hours?"

D'Alembert spoke in a storm now.

"Done, gentlemen. Think fast."

The orders followed faster.

"Com, break off. All arrays down. Ahead one-third. Dive."

With that *Adresteia* slipped deeper beneath the waves, dove deep in the wine-dark sea.

Within minutes of transmission's end Devlin was summoned from his waiting to find the four men facing him from a large circular table. Auslander and Mann were side by side, forming its center, most distant from him. Collier and Shaw flanked them, were nearest to Devlin.

Auslander greeted him.

"Sorry to have had to keep you waiting so long, Admiral. We have a problem, I'm afraid. A very grave problem—with one of our Trident submarines—*Adresteia.*"

Devlin was utterly noncommittal.

"So I understood, Mr. Secretary."

"Yes. Well, we've been trying to piece this together here for the last several hours. Our best guess is that the captain seems to have misread our intent on some orders."

Devlin seemed skeptical.

"D'Alembert, sir?"

Admiral Shaw, the Chief of Naval Operations, and Devlin's immediate superior, answered him.

"Yes, d'Alembert."

Auslander resumed his presentation of the matter.

"Admiral, nothing said here leaves this room—that is to be understood. Last week I personally gave verbal orders—in the CNO's office, with Admiral Shaw present—to Captain d'Alembert. He was to retarget three missiles on new Soviet coordinates—ASATs. We had learned they had developed a beam-type system that we felt gave them a viable no-war war option."

The Secretary of Defense allowed himself a brief pause before continuing.

"At midnight tonight we received a message from d'Alembert that he would launch in precisely one hundred twenty hours, that he would make no further contact with the command network, and that we should take necessary precautions against a Soviet response."

Devlin made a considerable effort to betray no reaction. He succeeded.

"With all respect, Mr. Secretary, why on earth would he do that?"

Mann answered him.

"We can only surmise, Devlin, but I think the logic of the situation is fairly clear. You can certainly appreciate the level of threat presented by this ASAT capability. So could d'Alembert. He knew our hands would be tied."

"You're suggesting, then, that d'Alembert has taken this into his own hands? I find that hard to accept, sir. D'Alembert is a loyal officer."

"That is precisely the point, Admiral. D'Alembert is a loyal officer. He must have understood our urgency over those ASATs. Even our fears."

Devlin considered this. He could see the truth in the possibility.

"You had better accept it, Admiral, because it has happened—and we need you to do something about it." It was Collier speaking to him now, the Army telling the Navy it had a problem. A big problem.

Shaw said nothing to Devlin for the moment. Auslander continued.

"It is a fact, Admiral. We have been told, simply,

plainly, that d'Alembert will launch in less than five days on a depressed trajectory, taking out those ASATs with a single strike. He has as much as told us that it's our game from that point. But he will take out that threat—and he is asking no one's permission to do so."

Devlin left his standing position, paced the space available to him. The four men watched him in silence.

Devlin weighed d'Alembert. Weighed the scenario his seniors had just presented him.

If d'Alembert decided a difficult thing had to be done, Devlin knew, he would do it. If he had concluded it was necessary to do this thing, to force them to save themselves, to force them to act . . . d'Alembert could do it.

Had done it.

Devlin turned to face them.

"He said no communications?"

"None," Mann answered.

"Not even immediately before launch?"

"Correct, Quenten," Shaw answered. "Damn it, we have a madman on our hands. Or a monster. We have to stop him."

"You can't stop him."

It was spoken with authority.

"I beg your pardon," Auslander said.

"Gentlemen, you are confronted by a Trident submarine, the most powerful single weapons system on the face of the earth—*Adresteia*, best of her class. More importantly, you are confronted by Alexander d'Alembert, her captain—the most able, determined man I know—particularly in a hard spot."

Devlin looked at them in turn.

"If d'Alembert is determined to launch, there is no power on heaven or earth that can stop him."

"Take the con, Charles, I want to think in private for a little while."

With that d'Alembert abruptly left the control room to Fox's command, traversed the short distance to his cabin.

He emerged one hour later.

"Charles, I've made a decision."

"Yes, Captain?"

"When we contact them again we will give them seventy-two hours to finalize our requirements. No more."

Fox thought this over carefully. "You really think they may be foolish enough to try something."

"Let's just say that I'm not foolish enough to give them much of a chance. Seventy-two hours after next contact."

Fox nodded.

"Okay, Skipper."

Mann spoke for the four of them.

"Listen, Devlin, we're in two separate dilemmas here. Firstly, we have the problem of d'Alembert. Secondly, we have the equal problem of keeping all this mess from the President."

"He doesn't know?"

"Not yet."

Devlin hesitated at this information.

"Christ, Devlin," Mann said, "think what it would mean if he knew a submarine commander had taken this into his own hands. It's like a nightmare."

Devlin saw Mann's point. He began once again to

pace the distance in measured fashion, speaking softly as he did so.

"The odds are terrible. D'Alembert could be anywhere in the Pacific and still hit his targets, though not on a depressed trajectory. He knows where our sonar emplacements are positioned on the ocean floor, our deployments, our procedures. *Adresteia* is deep-diving, fast, maneuverable, quiet. There is no way to localize a hunt. No way to use a large force."

"No, we don't want that," Mann said. "We have to handle this ourselves. It's our problem. Not the President's."

Devlin considered. Reconsidered.

Shook his head.

"I just don't see it."

Mann fixed Devlin with his eyes.

"You *will* find a way, Devlin. I want a report in six hours. You will find a way or I swear to God, if it is the last thing I do, I will *ruin* you."

Devlin seemed to consider this, too. He held Mann's eyes, then took in the others as well, Auslander last of all.

"Gentlemen, I will do what I can. You'll have your report within six hours. I will make my final recommendations at that time. But bear in mind, I am not a miracle worker. I am not prescient. I cannot do the impossible."

"Make it possible," Mann said.

Devlin shrugged, started for the door.

"I'll see what I can do," he said. Then, as if it were an afterthought, he turned back toward them.

"Oh. By the way. Don't threaten me again. Ever."

He looked at Mann.

"Understood?"
"Understood."

A short time after Devlin left the meeting, *Orcus* prepared to surface in the polar night. The Russian submarine had found a suitable spot in the ice after a false attempt, broken through. Hansen laboriously positioned them within a hundred meters of the Soviet vessel, then brought them up with a crash of ice.

Orcus's sail stood above the ice, swept by the winter winds. Hansen ordered contact made with the command net, their position reported.

"Position noted, Skipper, linking through the command net now."

The message that awaited *Orcus* leaped to their situation display, glowing red before their silence.

> —YOU WILL CEASE ALL OPERATIONS PENDING MY PERSONAL ORDERS.
> —STAND BY.
> —DEVLIN.

Orcus was in it.

CHAPTER 10

Devlin could well appreciate the need for the most absolute discretion, for sharply restricting the number of people who knew of *Adresteia*'s renegade status. Accordingly, he limited himself to calling in only his two most senior staff members, Brown and Wingarde.

While awaiting their arrival he immersed himself in the tactical situation. He had been commander of several boats in his time, but the last few years of his career had seen him surrounded by strategic considerations. Projecting. Planning. Lobbying. It was time for him, now, to turn back to the particulars, to details.

It had been his instinctive decision to alert *Orcus*. An immediate gut reaction. While Devlin was no grizzled salt who moved on instinct alone, was instead very much a product of his technological time who knew his computerized analyses and projections intimately, he knew, too, the value of trusting his subconscious analyses as well as his conscious ones. Alerting *Orcus* had been such a response, sudden and inescapable.

He stood, for a time, silent, in the situation room near his office, thinking it through. There were a number of elements present here that he did not like—not least of which were the need for secrecy and the very fact of d'Alembert, his friend, having gone renegade. D'Alembert had served under him and Devlin knew him very well. Knew him to be an extraordinarily capable officer.

Brown arrived, followed shortly by Wingarde, both men hastily dressed. Devlin briefed the two men while he shaved, outlining the situation in a crisp, factual fashion that left no room for doubt or hesitation. They had two hours to thrash it through, see if there were indeed an effective way to stop *Adresteia*. Destroy her. Before she destroyed them.

They settled down to it.

Angelo Coppi looked at his captain.

"Wonder what's up," he said.

"Damned if I know," was the reply. "Whatever it is, it's a little strange. This is a strange way to get new orders."

"Yeah."

"Well, I guess we'll know when they're ready to tell us—not before."

"Hurry up and wait, you mean."

"Pretty much."

Hansen looked, then, at the displayed numbers indicating hull stresses from the ice around them.

"Let's take her down a few inches," he said. "Just ease her off a little."

Orcus settled cautiously, easing the pressure.

"I know," Hansen said. "I'm an old woman. I worry. Angel, what do you say to a bit of a game with our good friends the Russians."

Coppi smiled.

"Why not? You want me to patch it up?"

"Sure. It'll pass the time."

"Okay, Skipper."

In short order *Orcus* put through a radio call to the silent Russian missile submarine that lay a hundred meters away in the cold winter night.

"Good day, Captain," Hansen said.

"Good day, Captain," came the virtually unaccented reply. "I should congratulate you on your skill."

"Thank you."

"Do you enjoy hunting in the Arctic?"

"It's challenging."

"I agree. It has other advantages as well."

"Really?"

"Yes. Always a plentiful supply of ice, which is reassuring."

Hansen laughed.

"Also," the Soviet commander continued, "there is usually an ample supply of American attack submarines—which I find slightly less reassuring."

"Yes, I can understand that, Captain," Hansen said, somewhat uncertain.

The etiquette of such situations was awkward. One of the ground rules was that one was seldom so rude as to inquire after the other vessel's name—or her captain's. It simply wasn't done.

"If I may ask, Captain," Hansen ventured, "will you be getting underway soon—just so we can coordinate our movements."

"I understand. No. Not for several hours, I expect. And you?"

"Probably the same."

"Very well, Captain. I will alert you if there is any likelihood of conflict in maneuvering."

"Thank you."

"Oh, Captain?"

"Yes?" Hansen said.

"Merry Christmas." The Russian laughed.

"Thanks. Same to you—I guess."

"Till we meet again, Captain."

The Soviet boat signed off. Hansen and Coppi found themselves amused by the awkward exchange. The Russian seemed all right.

"I'll tell you one thing, Skipper."

"Yes?"

"His English is a hell of a lot better than my Russian."

Hansen nodded. "Too bad he's not a little better with that boat of his."

"We do have the advantage, Skipper. We usually do."

"I intend to keep it that way."

The first light of morning fell through Devlin's office window.

"Look, our hands are tied behind our backs. There's just not very much we can offer under these circumstances," Brown said.

"I agree. But we have to do something," Wingarde responded.

Devlin thought for a second. He was tired.

"Well, of course we can do *something*," he said. "The question is, can we do anything that has a chance—instead of provoking d'Alembert to act even more hastily."

"Granted," Wingarde said. "Do you have a clear indication from the Chiefs and the Secretary with respect to what risk they think acceptable—with respect to the President and respect to provoking d'Alembert to launch just that much sooner?"

"They place a very high priority on keeping this to

themselves. As far as the risk of provoking a launch is concerned, they'll accept that. What is there to lose? If he's going to launch on those ASATs then he's going to launch. One day or two won't make much difference."

"Then there isn't an awful lot of help we can give them," Brown said. "The confidentiality is the limiting factor—and *Adresteia*'s parameters."

"And those are some tight parameters," Devlin acknowledged. "Without even a means of localizing the situation . . ."

"What are you going to recommend, then, Quenten?"

"The one option we have, I suppose. Not that it's likely to matter. It's the only way we have a chance of handling the situation, though."

"Mann's going to bitch a fit," Wingarde observed. "What are you going to tell him?"

"I am going to tell him," Devlin said, "to pray a lot. And keep his head down."

Mann woke from his nap on the office couch. He needed a shave. And a shower. He stabbed at the intercom.

"Charlie?"

"Yes, General?"

"Get me some coffee, would you?"

"Sure thing, General."

When the aide brought it, he found Mann already in the shower.

"Get through to Hughes, yet?" he asked the aide.

"They're working on a computer analysis of the new antenna array now. They'll call back when they have the numbers."

"Good. How did they sound?"

"Well, frankly, sir, I think they can give us something that will enable NavSynch 7 to provide us with a bearing of some sort—but I don't know how good it will be—you know the problems with a laser carrier beam."

Mann nodded. He knew.

"If it's any help at all, we'll go for it."

"Do you want the Air Force Space Shuttle put on immediate standby for launch, then?"

Mann considered their time window.

"How long till the people at Hughes have the numbers for the new localizer array?"

"A couple of hours, I'd guess."

Mann made his decision.

"They sounded reasonably optimistic. Call the base and have them put on full standby."

"Very well, General."

"Charlie?"

"Sir?"

"Keep CIA posted."

"Right."

Devlin had a few minutes to spare before reporting to Mann with his conclusion. Not long enough to get the sleep he needed.

He strolled over to the situation room where he studied the shifting patterns of the displays, the men and women at their posts. Myriad bits of data fed those displays, scanned and shuttle-sorted by the thousands. None of it could tell him where to look for *Adresteia*. Or where to find d'Alembert. Where he was and—more importantly—why. Somewhere in the Pacific. That little he knew. Somewhere deep in the greatest expanse of water on the globe, in a vessel optimized for avoiding any form of detection.

He didn't have a hound's chance in hell and he knew it.

He turned to one of the men.

"What's your current on the Bering Strait?"

Mann phoned to Devlin to tell him that he would meet him in Devlin's office. Five minutes before he left to negotiate the interlocking halls of the Pentagon, his phone rang. It was the man from Hughes.

"General Mann?"

"Yes."

"I can give you five hundred nautical radius resolution with a point five error probable. Ready in five hours for launch vehicle."

Mann thought.

"That's not wildly impressive."

"General, I can't give you wildly impressive on four hours' notice."

Mann grunted acknowledgment.

"All right, I'll go with it. Liaison with my people directly."

"Okay, General."

The man hung up. Mann was deeply disappointed. He had really hoped for something an order of magnitude better. But there was nothing to be done for it. He would take what he could get.

It was better than nothing.

Hansen had begun to get seriously restless waiting for new orders. The ice that surrounded *Orcus* was thin, really, so that it posed no real problem—but Hansen had been operating in the Arctic for some years and knew all too well how suddenly a stable situation could become unstable.

Each slight shift of the ice echoed through the spaces of the submarine with the unnerving cry of cold ice on cold steel alloy.

"Angel, try and get some rest. At this rate we may be waiting till spring—not that that will make much difference. Except for a little daylight."

The Soviet submarine waited, too, though *Orcus* had no way of knowing why. Hansen's guess was simply that they hoped to learn something from *Orcus*. He had given orders from the first to keep a close watch for anything foolish. He now ordered the watch kept very sharp. *Orcus* had her share of sensors, and it was virtually inconceivable that the Russians would do anything imprudent. But it was best to be alert.

More likely than not the Soviet skipper preferred not to leave the area first, knowing *Orcus* might well shadow him. Too, they probably hoped to acquire acoustical signature data on *Orcus*. Hansen smiled at the thought. There were defenses for that, too.

"Any messages imminent?"

"Sorry, Skipper. Nothing."

"Shit."

Mann walked into Devlin's office, took a seat.

"So, what have you got?" he asked.

"Not a great deal," Devlin said. "It's a very big ocean, General."

"Call me Mal."

"Fine. I'll do that."

Devlin pushed his chair back from the desk, peered at Mann over its expanse.

"Mal, you want this on a low profile. A very low profile."

"Correct. And that means problems."

"That means, to put it bluntly, that there is no way I can order a wide-area search of any effectiveness—not that it would be likely to produce results. *Adresteia* is as quiet as death, and d'Alembert is not likely to do anything that will make the job easier as he gets into position to launch on the ASATs."

"He doesn't have to be 'in position' with the missile range he has to work with," Mann observed.

"No. Not really. A six-thousand-mile range is more than enough. He pays a price in reduced accuracy if he opts for range on a depressed trajectory, but with ten warheads per target he can afford it. You're right, Mal, he could be anywhere."

"I know that. We both know that. What can you do for me?"

Devlin looked scrupulously out the window.

"Have you considered letting this simply take its course, preparing to react once d'Alembert launches?"

"Not for a moment."

"Maybe you should, Mal. It may come to that."

Mann was now presented with a dilemma of considerable magnitude. He considered, against Shaw's earlier advice, telling Devlin the truth. Quickly decided against it.

This was getting increasingly complex.

"The ASATs are an enormous threat," he said, "of a kind that is too subtle for the civilian leadership to fully appreciate—ever. The threat is real enough to me that I could consider letting it play out d'Alembert's way—if there were no other considerations. But there are."

Devlin nodded. Mann continued.

"The fact of the matter is that the President doesn't know a thing yet—just a small leak about the ASATs that we had Auslander make yesterday. He knows about the beam-ASATs, and about the retargeting—but not about d'Alembert's going off the deep end. Quenten, we had Auslander make that leak for the sole purpose of sounding out Elliott's reaction to the threat, to see if he'd perceive it in the same dramatic light we do. Obviously, though he takes it seriously, he doesn't. And he won't. It's a matter of perspective. So what it comes down to in the end is that we have to find a way to put an end to d'Alembert's threat before we dare approach Elliott. We're all on the line by association if d'Alembert launches."

"You're probably right," Devlin said, seeing Mann's point. "Well, I can't do a great deal, really. I can correlate any lucky findings from ASW ships or aircraft on routine patrol, but we can't mount a search under these circumstances. As I said, I'm not certain that option would have that much to recommend it even if it were open to us."

"D'Alembert is that good?"

"Without question."

"You have implied that you do have something."

"I can give you one attack sub. *Orcus*. Maybe."

"Explain."

"Okay. I wouldn't risk going in on *Ardesteia* with anything but an attack sub. It's the only chance we have of taking him sufficiently off his guard to take him out of action before he can launch. It isn't certain. It's still a chance—but it makes sense."

"Why only one boat?"

"Because you want to keep this from the President

A. P. Kobryn

so we don't look any worse than we have to. Because communications with a boat in action are out of the question. Because our ELF is very limited. I can't advise risking an uncoordinated attack. It could become chaos. And d'Alembert would use any chaos to his own advantage—very effectively, I might add."

Mann nodded in clear agreement.

"Why *Orcus*?" he asked.

"*Orcus* is the best boat I have. The decisive factor though, isn't *Orcus*, but her captain—Russell Hansen."

"Good?"

"More than good. A killer. More than that. He can take orders."

Devlin looked out the window again for a moment, turned back to Mann.

"More than that," he said. "Hansen was d'Alembert's exec for four years. They're close. He knows d'Alembert like a brother. He can think like him. That could make all the difference."

Mann swiftly considered the factors before reaching his decision.

"All right, Admiral. We go with *Orcus*. Now, why the 'maybe'?"

"*Orcus* is in the Arctic Ocean. A long way from the Pacific. I need time."

Mann knew that that would be difficult. Might be next to impossible. He considered carefully.

"I'll get you whatever time you need."

"There's another problem," Devlin said. "The Bering Strait was a mess last winter and it's worse this year. The ice is freakishly bad, the bottom is shallow, the currents seem to have shifted."

"And the Bering Strait is the only way."

126

Devlin nodded.

"Precisely how bad are conditions?"

"There's a chance. A chance worth taking—but a long way from certain."

"You'd still advise against risking any other boat?"

"Yes."

"Then we'll take the chance," Mann said, rising from his seat.

"I'll get on with it, then."

"Good. Quenten, I know this is especially rough for you—with d'Alembert and all. I know you expected great things from him."

"Yeah. That was a long time ago, now, Mal. Yesterday."

"Hang in there. I may have some good news for you on the location problem in a day or so."

Devlin looked at Mann. What did he have up his sleeve?

"I always appreciate good news, General."

"So do I. Have *Orcus* make all possible speed. I'll see what I can do to buy you time."

"Please do. Time is the most important thing I don't have."

CHAPTER 11

Devlin lost no time in arranging for the call to be put through to *Orcus*. The arrangements were already made, the securely coded voice link was ready. Hansen was told to take the call in private, patched through to his cabin. He did so.

Devlin was to the point.

"Russ, I have some very painful orders for you."

"Sir?"

"I need *Orcus* to make an all-out effort to get through to the Bering Strait and into the Pacific. With all possible speed."

"Sure thing, Admiral."

"Can you do it?"

"Well, I can give it one hell of a try."

Devlin paused.

"Russ, there's a reason for this haste. I . . . we need you to hunt down *Adresteia*."

There was a long pause.

"I don't understand. What kind of an exercise. . . ."

"Not an exercise, Captain. The real thing. *Adresteia* has gone renegade."

Hansen did not, could not, believe what he was hearing.

"Renegade? D'Alembert? Renegade?"

Devlin was firm.

"Captain, you will be fully briefed if and when you reach the Pacific. For the present it *will* suffice to say that *Adresteia* has become the gravest possible threat to the security of the United States and that the only way to end that threat is to destroy her."

There was a very long pause.

"I don't know what to say to that, Admiral."

"Neither do I, Russ, but you'd better start getting accustomed to the idea. This is not an exercise, joke, or test. We desperately need *Adresteia* taken out. You are the only man I have who has a chance—precisely because you were d'Alembert's exec. You know him. The fate of a hell of a lot of people depends on you, Hansen. Do you read me?"

Hansen's reply was muted. "I read you, sir."

Devlin hesitated before returning to the matter at hand.

"Look, Russ, we've got a first-class nightmare on our hands. Now you're in it, too, and our only way out is sinking *Adresteia*. The only way, Russ."

"I guess I'll . . . have to see what I can do."

"You're a good officer, Hansen. We're all counting on you."

"Right."

"You'll have your final orders when you reach the Pacific. Now get cracking."

"Aye, aye, sir."

Fox rubbed the sleep from his eyes.

"So," he said, "we'll know one way or the other in the next few hours."

"I'm not so certain of that, Charles. But I think we'll have an idea."

Fox nodded sleepily, fighting off a yawn.

"Wishful thinking on my part, I guess. Suppose, Alex, that they basically concede. Can we consider in more detail where we go from there? We've only been able to paint it in broad terms, so far."

"I don't really see how we can do a great deal better then that at this point, Charles. Do you?"

"No, not really. Frankly, though, I prefer to try to think about the more optimistic side of the equation—not that it's exactly a daydream."

D'Alembert saw the point of this. They had a long way to go.

"Well," he said, "Morgan is in Zurich, as you know. They're free to arrange the transfer of funds in whatever manner they find most acceptable—we know they'll have to do something to keep it invisible from the GAO and the President. Which shouldn't be too difficult, really, considering their access and the comparatively modest sum involved—the cost of one F-14. Morgan will take it from there, she'll have worked it out with a banker by this time."

"If they get . . . funny?"

"With Morgan? They won't—I'm sure of it. They're not that foolhardy. It would be suicidal. They know I'd have the sense to arrange elementary precautions, at least in terms of key words, and I'm counting on their common sense."

"Their 'enlightened self-interest'?"

"A fair way to put it."

"I think you're okay on that assumption. Also, Switzerland is the last place in the world to risk getting daring. Once they know she's there—they probably already do—that, alone, would put them off. Their risks would be enormous."

"Out of all sane proportion as long as we're still out here, waiting for confirmation."

"When Morgan's satisfied, she gives them the key word to relay to us."

"And if she isn't, it will be another word, and they'll know that, and know there's no way of knowing in advance. It's simple and basically fail-safe."

"Do you think we're assuming too much intelligence and common sense?"

"I can't see them not recognizing the pattern of it instantly."

"Okay," Fox said, "then at that point we move on to putting Michaels ashore for additional insurance. We'll be in position by then."

"I don't see a problem there."

"Neither do I. That will take care of the transition to the long term. The long term, though . . ."

" 'In the long term, we are all dead,' " d'Alembert quoted. "It simply depends on how far we extend the curve."

"True."

"But not very reassuring?"

"Not terribly."

"Well, Charles, I think we have a fair chance. The income from the money will provide us with the funds for security arrangements and new lives for those of us who know about the original mission. We've kept any real knowledge from the crew as a whole, for their own good, and the Chiefs will keep a watch on that end for their own benefit."

"And if they ever make a false move we can go public."

"Yes. And they know that. And they know the consequences."

"It could get sticky if someone gets hot-headed, Alex."

"So could World War Three."

Fox nodded.

"Look, Charles, it's an accurate comparison in a number of ways. As you observed earlier, I think, it's a deterrent situation—who would perceive that better than the Joint Chiefs. But we have a fair chance—maybe even a good chance—as long as the risk of their exposure is more unthinkable to them than merely swallowing their pride and conceding the point to us—which is, essentially, what's involved here. Pride."

"A mutual accommodation, then."

"Yes."

Fox looked at the wall chronometer, its liquid crystal shifting with the time.

"Aren't you worried about Morgan and the kids?"

"How could I not be. I'm worried about all of us. Morgan's a damn capable woman. We can count on her."

"Okay, Skipper. So we wait out Mann. I'm assuming he's the central figure."

"Not necessarily. He could be a stalking horse for Auslander or someone else."

"Somehow, Alex, I can't see Malcolm Mann as anyone's stalking horse."

"Neither can I."

Hansen stormed into the control room of *Orcus* like a man possessed.

"Engineering, can you give me flank speed?"

There was an astonished pause from engineering.

"Uh, sure, Captain. In about five minutes. I can give you full power now if you need it."

"Okay, stand by."

Coppi looked at Hansen.

"Uh, Skipper," he said, "the Russian . . ."

"I don't give a damn about the Russian. Get me a plot for the Bering Strait."

There was no denying Hansen's urgency.

"Right on it, Skipper."

"Communications, tell our Russian friends we're leaving the area."

"Aye, aye, sir."

"Diving officer, I want down."

With that they began the process of maneuvering, submerging beneath the ice, working clear of the Soviet missile submarine.

Hansen cousulted the tac/nav display. Their new course was clearly delineated.

"Engineering, come to full power."

"Aye, aye, sir."

Once again Coppi looked at his captain. One did *not* make full speed right under the Russians' collective noses.

Hansen was impatient, but reconsidered.

"Engineering, amend that. Give me one-third ahead for the next few minutes."

"Aye, aye, sir, ahead one-third."

Coppi relaxed visibly.

"Angel, we've got to get moving. Fast. I can't be too delicate with these scow-driving Russians."

"Sure thing, Skipper."

"Sonar?"

"Nothing, Captain. He's lying still. Listening."

"Okay."

"Wait a minute, Skipper . . . he's beginning to bleed off some ballast. Easing down, quiet like."

"Shit. We have a nice little trade-off to make here. Engineering, go to two-thirds. Sonar, see what you can do to fox their readings."

"Aye, aye, Skipper."

Several minutes passed as *Orcus* came to speed. Made distance.

"How's he doing, sonar?"

"He's coming on, Captain, accelerating. Fairly slow at the moment."

"Keep on him. Helm, start us down, give me three down bubble initially. I'm going to want three hundred."

"Aye, aye, sir, three down initial, making for three zero zero meters."

The captain turned to his executive officer.

"Angel, what would you suggest?"

"If we want a chance of throwing him off our course I'd try ninety for a while."

"Agreed. Helm, come to zero nine five. Give me full ahead."

The orders were duly acknowledged.

"Three hundred meters, Captain."

Hansen considered.

"Sonar, be ready to throw everything you've got at him on my mark."

"Okay, Skipper."

"I'm going to want flank speed on that same mark, gentlemen. Helm, at that point you will come hard about to one seven eight."

The orders were confirmed and understood.

"Standing by, Skipper."

Orcus seemed to concentrate, preparing to lunge forward. They ran a very real chance of showing the Russian just what they could do, but they would have to accept that risk.

"Mark."

Orcus began her rush for the Pacific in earnest.

Auslander and the Joint Chiefs had agreed to let Mann handle the next communication with d'Alembert on his own in order that they might spend the day at home, both getting some needed rest and attempting to maintain a semblance of normal activities. Mann would keep a single hard copy of the electronic interchange so that they might consult it if they wished. He would then destroy that single copy.

They met briefly once again that morning before separating. The meeting was held in Auslander's office this time and he opened it with a question.

"Should we pay him off?"

"Are you kidding?" Collier asked.

"It would buy us time," Auslander replied.

"Oh. I see your point. Sorry, Auslander."

"Quite all right. In any case, it makes sense to me. Even if we handle this as efficiently as we have to, which won't be easy, we will need time. We may as well buy d'Alembert's trust with a little money."

"We do need time," Mann said. "More than I thought. Devlin strongly advises against anything more radical than sending out a single attack submarine. He's not entirely sanguine even about that."

"I'm not surprised, under these circumstances," the CNO said. "As I said, d'Alembert's good. And it's a big ocean."

Mann glared at him.

"Nothing personal, Dave, but if I hear that little litany one more time today I am going to break someone's back."

Everyone smiled slightly awkwardly.

"I see your point," Shaw said.

"Anything we can do?" Collier asked.

"I think so," Mann said. "The main problem is initial localization. I've been talking to the people at Hughes. If it works out, I'll let you know."

Collier looked a little uneasy.

"I don't know any delicate way to put this, but I've been thinking security and I've been at least idly wondering if we shouldn't consider going after this on the other end—the wife."

"I vehemently disagree, General," Auslander interrupted. "As long as he's out there with those missiles aimed at our jugular, the last thing I relish is some melodramatic, risky business in Switzerland. We have to handle him at sea or not at all. The same thing goes, as far as I'm concerned, if we fail to stop him."

"Let's not admit failure quite yet," Mann said. "I know I'm not ready to, for one."

They all agreed with this. They did not want to fail. It would be the end of them. But they had, it seemed, no weapon but *Orcus*—which didn't seem like much. One attack submarine. Still in the Arctic.

"I want to bring CIA in a little closer on this thing," Collier said quietly.

"How much closer?" Shaw asked.

"So they have more of a personal stake. I think that's prudent. I'd like to have them put a watch on d'Alembert's wife. A close watch. That would give us some flexibility with them."

Mann appeared uneasy in turn.

"I don't much care for it," he said, "but it makes good sense to tie them closer to us. As long as they are *very* clear that it is surveillance only. And I do mean only."

"I completely concur," Collier said. "I expect to make that crystal clear for them."

"Okay," Mann said. "Any last thoughts for the moment on how I should handle d'Alembert?"

Auslander was the first to respond.

"I think we should put it to him that we're conceding—while kicking and dragging our heels."

"Agreed. But not too heavy."

"Fair enough."

Shaw put in his last thoughts next. "Emphasize the difficulty of our transferring the money without blowing our cover. He'll buy that."

Mann made a note to himself.

"I think it would be generally useful," Collier said, "to play to the point, to at least suggest it, that we have to play this very quiet and very close—he's premising his actions on that. If it's not overdone, it should reassure him, confirm his judgment. And it's largely the truth—which never hurts."

Mann made another note.

"Any other last thoughts at this point?" he asked.

There were none. They were all tired.

Auslander spoke for them all. "We know you know how to handle this as well as any of us could, General. You can reach us if you need us."

Then one last question from Shaw, addressing what was, for them, the main point of the exercise.

"Can you get *Orcus* the time she'll need."

Mann nodded.

"I have to."

* * *

Morgan d'Alembert was in the bathroom of the small suite, brushing her hair. The children had spent most of the day playing with their new toys—Jennifer with a radio-controlled racing car and Joshua with a new microcomputer. She had decided to indulge them somewhat this year in order to keep them occupied.

Jennifer knocked as she had been taught, entered.

"Mother, why are we here this year instead of home?"

Jennifer could be persistent.

"I told you before, dear, your father thought it would be nice this year if, instead of being home all alone without him, we went on vacation. Then we'll all come home together."

This did not appear to entirely satisfy Jennifer.

"Is there anything wrong with Father?"

Morgan did not like to lie to the children.

"Of course not."

There were exceptions.

"All right, Mother."

From her tone it was clear that the child was still not entirely satisfied, but she left her mother, for the moment, to her hair and the empty room.

Mann took the communication from d'Alembert through the same channel he had selected earlier. Again the words glowed on the screen as the operator typed them, as d'Alembert replied through his operator. There were infinite limitations of lost nuance to this, Mann knew, but he had decided for it.

The first words from d'Alembert stared at him as he strode into the room, wearily took a seat.

"Are you prepared to discuss specifics?"

"Yes."

"Will you call off the mission?"

Mann did not hesitate.

"We will," he said to the screen.

"No other modality will be employed?"

"No."

"If you were to select alternate unauthorized means, you realize I would expose you."

Mann was more weary than he had realized.

"Yes," he said. The operator typed it in.

D'Alembert was persistent, Mann thought. He would not let up on him.

"As simple as that?" he asked Mann next.

"As simple as that, damn it," Mann said, then immediately amended himself to the aide at the keyboard—"Delete the 'damn it.'"

"Why?" d'Alembert nagged at him.

"You leave us no choice, Captain."

"I hadn't meant to, General. Very well. You will inform the President of what you have done."

Mann sat on the edge of his chair in fury.

"No. I will not," he said to the operator. Then, to himself, "Go to hell, d'Alembert."

"It is the best guarantee of my men's safety," came d'Alembert's response.

Mann was furious, but it didn't matter because only the words were relayed through the command net. His anger stayed in the room with him.

"Captain, you know perfectly well that you would not simply accept our word about informing the President—and you also know that you would not be able to trust any communication link made available to you by me. We both know this."

"It seems we do. The President, however, could initiate a link over the executive command authority channel. I could rely on such a link as being authentic."

Mann became, if possible, even more angry.

"You are pushing too far, Captain. I cannot go that far and survive. Think again."

Mann was holding his ground. D'Alembert had expected as much. If d'Alembert insisted on Mann's informing the President of the truth, Mann would refuse—and the only choice left d'Alembert would be to actually launch *Adresteia*'s missiles.

There was a long hesitation in the exchange before d'Alembert's words appeared again on the screen.

"Very well, General. My crew and I, however, would also prefer to survive. I require, then, your pledge of absolute secrecy on this entire matter as well as your abandonment of your illegal and unilateral action. You will not harass my crew or their families. Ever. You will transfer the necessary funds to the Swiss account as a token of your sincerity. If you do not . . ."

"You are understood, Captain."

"When will you be able to transfer the money?"

Mann could see now how it would all end. He had been playing for this one seemingly minor point.

"I need time to arrange it," he said.

"You have forty-eight hours," was the immediate reply.

"Not enough." Mann paused then, letting d'Alembert wait. "We must, I repeat, must be able to make the transfer secretly. I must work around channels. I need time."

D'Alembert let him wait before responding.

"How much time?"

"One week."

It was as much as Mann dared hope for.

"That is a very long time, General. What do you intend to do with it?"

Mann thought quickly—how did d'Alembert expect him to react?

"Do not test me, d'Alembert," he said.

Again there was a long pause in the transmission.

"I will consider it. Next contact in twenty-four hours."

Adresteia broke the link.

Mann walked out of the room exhausted. Keeping his own counsel.

He had held him off for the moment. How long a moment would it be? Enough?

He headed home.

In vertical arc the honey descended dreamily from the spoon, swirled itself into the teacup.

"Damn. You okay, fingers?"

She set aside the squeezed-out tea bag, settled into the *Times*. She knew well enough what the *Post* would look like, so it could wait.

And how was the competition this morning? Fair to middling, thank you. It was a thin edition. The holiday, she remembered.

She took a container of milk from the refrigerator, added the necessary portion to her tea, set it on the table and returned to the paper.

The small apartment was still in the morning when the telephone rang. She answered reluctantly, recognized the voice when she picked up the receiver.

"Ms. Worthington?"

"Yes?"

"I may have something of interest to you."

"Where do you want to meet?"

"Same as before."

"It's been a while."

"I know. How soon can you make it?"

"Thirty minutes."

"I'll be waiting."

She left the paper open on the table beside her tea, took a last sip.

It would be cold before she was back.

CHAPTER 12

Devlin rang the bell of Auslander's Georgetown house late that day. Auslander answered, showed him to the first-floor study.

"Have a seat, Admiral."

"Thanks."

"Can I get you anything? A cup of coffee?"

"Tea, if you have any."

"Certainly."

Auslander left to fetch Devlin a cup of tea. Devlin waited, studied the furnishings. Simple. In good taste. Auslander returned.

"I asked you to drop by, Admiral, because, as Secretary of Defense, my responsibilities are somewhat different than those of the Joint Chiefs—as you well know. I want your honest evaluation of the situation, and I thought that was better accomplished if we met in private."

"I understand that, Mr. Secretary. What, precisely, would you like to know?"

Auslander took a seat.

"I want an honest estimate of *Orcus*'s chances of stopping *Adresteia* from firing on those ASATs. One not influenced by the fact that your superiors are staring you in the face, effectively demanding that you perform—even if it's impossible."

"Mr. Secretary, I am very seldom guilty of that particular fault. I sure as hell hope I wasn't this morning. I wouldn't want anyone getting needlessly optimistic."

"The chances?"

Devlin placed his cup on the table beside him. "The chances," he said, "are not very good. I frankly believe that there is a very real risk in sending *Orcus* against *Adresteia*."

"What level of risk?"

Devlin shrugged. Stroked idly at his neatly trimmed beard.

"As I said this morning, Mr. Secretary, *Adresteia*—aside from being next to impossible to locate—can react very quickly to any threat. She can launch. She can defend herself. There is a risk involved—but, since d'Alembert has said that he'll launch anyway, it doesn't make a great deal of difference, does it?"

"No. It doesn't," Auslander replied. "Devlin, is there any effective means *Orcus* could employ to signal *Adresteia*—to call her off, to pass a message?"

Devlin answered with authority. "Certainly, once she's in range. Of course, that would reveal her presence and position to *Adresteia*, and would leave her no chance of operating effectively against her—or surviving, if it came to that."

"You're implying d'Alembert would attack *Orcus*."

Devlin smiled sardonically.

"Instantly, Mr. Secretary. Instantly and without hesitation. He'll defend himself. D'Alembert isn't a schoolboy—if he's decided to do this thing, to take out those ASATs on his own, he's also thought about the possible countermoves and consequences. He'll do as he sees fit. Don't doubt that for even a moment."

"Then there's nothing we can do."

"I never said that. I said we could risk sending out *Orcus*. Turning Russell Hansen loose is not doing nothing by any stretch of my imagination."

"But you don't give him much of a chance of *finding Adresteia*."

"Well, if you'd like, I'll call up every piece of ASW equipment I've got in the entire Pacific. Just say the word. But the odds are still fairly poor, even with that—and, of course, the President would soon know."

"That won't do, Devlin. It won't do at all."

Devlin considered the next question carefully.

"Well, that raises another question for me, Mr. Secretary. Have you thought of reconsidering? You might be a good deal better off in some ways if the President knew d'Alembert had gone renegade on you. There would be a lot of egg on your face, but it would mean far greater flexibility."

Auslander seemed disturbed at this question, as Devlin had rather expected. The Secretary of Defense rose from his chair, paced the room a few times before answering.

"I've thought about it, Devlin. A lot. More, I'm sure, than you or the CNO or Mann or Collier. But I can't see my way to it."

"Political considerations?"

"You might say that."

"I would say that. I understand your position. You want to keep your noses clean, provide the President with deniability—which he may very well need if *Adresteia* destroys three Russian antisatellite installations. Which he may also need if we stop her, but it turns out to be messy—in which case there is going to be a *lot* of investigating going on."

"You're not telling me anything I don't already know, Devlin."

"No, but I am telling you that I know it, too."

Auslander saw.

"At precisely what level would you peg the chances, Devlin?"

"I don't like to put a number on it. This is hardly a quantifiable matter."

"I need *some* idea."

Devlin sighed.

"Well, if you need an idea in fixed numbers, I'd give you one chance in ten. Mann mumbled something secretive about some variety of localization assistance—which, I'm sure, will be crude. If he can do that, it would bring the chances to about that level—in my judgment."

Auslander was appalled. "One in ten?" he echoed.

"If I have to put a number on it."

"Christ."

Auslander returned to his easy chair, took a sip of cold coffee.

"You mean to tell me," he said quietly, "that the chances are at least ten to one that d'Alembert will actually launch those missiles."

"Yes. I do."

Collier answered the telephone, rubbing his left eye, grumbling from his interrupted nap.

"Collier," he barked.

"Smith here," the voice answered.

"Oh. Smith. What have you got for me?"

"Well, General, I don't think you should be too concerned about the d'Alembert woman. We've been aware of her movements for some time—since she left the country, in fact. We're on top of it."

"Good," Collier said, relieved, "but surveillance only, mind you. That's essential."

Smith's voice responded with a good-humored laugh.

"Don't worry, General, CIA has no interest in getting itself enmeshed in this affair of yours. This is strictly your party and we want no part of it. We're just keeping our eyes open."

"Make sure it stays that way."

Collier hung up, phoned Shaw. The CNO took some time to answer.

"Shaw here."

"Dave, Collier. What do you think about the Company on this?"

Shaw seemed to be considering it. Collier idly tapped his pen on the desk top.

"They won't end-run us. They'd score a few points if they spilled their guts to the President, but it could very easily blow up in their faces, too. Healthier for all concerned—even CIA—if it stays in the family."

"Okay. Just wanted another opinion."

"Any time."

Collier thought about it for a while after hanging up. They had to be very, very careful. Anyone who might conceivably want to reach the President he wanted to know about—preferably before they even knew themselves. The number was now at twenty-three by his count. Not bad, considering.

* * *

Elliott had put off calling the Secretary of State for most of the afternoon. Somehow he didn't expect any unexpected insights from Moore. Finally, he had no choice.

"Yes, Mr. President, I've given it a great deal of thought. My recommendation is that we bring the matter of the ASATs up at next week's round of the arms negotiations."

"Isn't that kind of a long way off?"

"I recognize that full well, sir. However, it seems to me, on considering the matter, that it would not be prudent, given current strategic levels, to attempt a Cuban scenario. I certainly don't believe we have that level of overwhelming force at this point, Mr. President."

"Go on."

"Since we have every reason to assume that the installations have been operable for some time, we have no reason to believe that the Soviets intend their imminent employment on our strategic satellites. Current tensions are moderate, but not severe."

"Agreed."

"Given that fact, I fail to see why we should be as easily alarmed as Secretary Auslander reports the strategic types to be. We must be firm, I agree; but I think it will be quite enough to confront them unexpectedly over the table. We can have our forces standing by at that point, lest they act hastily. It seems to me far and away the best course and it offers the added advantage of giving the Joint Chiefs more than enough time in the next week to hang themselves."

Elliott pondered this message.

"Well, Mr. Secretary," he said, "I'm afraid that that thought does bother me a little bit."

148

"Letting them hang themselves?"

"Yes. They need watching over."

"You have Auslander to keep watch over them for you."

"True. . . ."

"At any rate, Mr. President, that is my recommendation. If I may, I would like to brief my people in the morning—at least to keep my option open."

"Very well, Mr. Secretary. I'll accept it as an option. But don't assume my decision until you have it."

"Of course not. The decision is yours, Mr. President."

Elliott hung up.

"You bet your ass it is," he said to himself.

Devlin was soon home again, again trying to get some sleep—at least to catch up. He phoned the situation room, asked if there were any reports from *Orcus*. There were none, as he had expected. There was little to do, really, for the next few hours, and there might be a great deal to do in the days to come. The best insurance he could think of at the moment was to get some sleep. An exhausted mind would be of little use to him.

Auslander's attitude in their discussion troubled him a little, but it was easily attributed to the tension between civilian and military leadership. Auslander didn't begin to trouble him in the same way as the fact of d'Alembert's going off the very end—and taking Fox and all of *Adresteia* with him.

Forcing him, in turn, to commit *Orcus* . . .

Enough. Rest.

* * *

She parked the car beside his in the deserted parking
lot. He was waiting. She went over, got in. She had
worked with him before, and she listened to him carefully now, making no notes, holding it in her head. He
was fairly high level, apparently, and well placed. He
had never been willing to talk about the nature of his
job, but his information had almost always been good.
He qualified, in her book, for whatever his motives
were, as a good source. Reliable.

One thing Worthington had often wondered about
was what portion of the information he had leaked
her in the past was meant to be leaked. Some of it, she
was certain. Equally certainly, not all of it.

He talked for twenty minutes, fencing with the
shadows. Then she stepped out and he drove off. She
was cold, wearing only a light jacket against the chill
air. She got into her car, started the engine for heat,
made the necessary notes, thought about what to do
next. The first thing to do was to phone her editor.

Mann met very late that day with Shaw. He was prin-
cipally concerned at the moment with the original mission and the fact of the beam-type ASATs. He wanted
to find a way to regain the initiative, though he
couldn't seem to see a way.

The two men had worked closely together for two
years. They were relaxed with one another, knew one
another's thought processes fairly well, reducing their
conversation at times to shorthand and ellipsis.

They spoke over a glass of wine, Mann, the older
man, speaking first.

"You're the Navy, so let's try the Navy first."

"Strategic?"

"I'd guess so."

"Okay. I didn't think we'd much care to drop in a team of commandos, so that makes it, from my end, widest conceivable option range: carrier aircraft, ballistic missiles, cruise missiles."

"Aircraft are out."

"Okay."

"Cruise is pretty well out of it. If we had something in inventory faster than Tomahawk . . . but we don't yet."

"I like the accuracy, though," Shaw said.

"True. We could consider using conventional warheads, which would be damn helpful."

"That it would."

"The problem, though," Mann said, "is the vulnerability to countermeasures. We'd have a chance of getting in undetected, but it's hardly a certainty."

"That does it in, really. Then we're back—no surprise—to where we were two weeks ago."

"Combined sortie?" Mann asked. "Reconnaissance aircraft to get their attention and cruise underneath?"

"Sounds better than the original except that it puts us in the wonderful world of coordinated operations. It'd sure be dramatic, though."

"Just thinking out loud."

"Sure thing. Look, Mal, we're back where we were when we started. We need credible deniability on the command authority. A sub is the only way to do that. We either go with a submarine or we take it up front. The command authority problem blows anything your Air Force could do out of the water, too. We're nowhere."

"Shit! There must be something."

"No, I don't think so, Mal. I don't think you think so, either. But we can kick it around. Personally, I think we're stuck with the ball as it lays."

"We handle d'Alembert as well as we can, then go up front on the ASATs to the President. Start over. Christ, I don't like that a bit. We know he won't do what has to be done, Dave."

"I know."

"I'm going to sound out CIA."

Shaw considered carefully.

"Are you really sure you want to do that?" he asked.

"No, but it's worth an inquiry."

Shaw sighed resignedly.

"Okay, Mal, but go easy with them, you hear?"

"You aren't telling me anything I don't already know."

Jean Worthington answered the phone.

"Jean?"

"Bill! Christ, I've been trying to get you all day."

"I know. It's a holiday, you know. Even for newspapermen. What's up?"

"I won't be in tomorrow. I'm on to something. I think."

"Care to discuss it with your father-confessor?"

"I don't know what I've got yet, really. It's pretty vague, but intriguing. I think it's worth a good feature. Give me a couple of days."

"Well . . . okay, you know what you're doing. But it better be worth it, Jean."

"Trust me. It'll be worth it."

CHAPTER 13

The Space Shuttle rose in a great column of flame, a fiery chariot if ever there was one. It ascended steeply, banking hard toward the horizon, shedding the solid-fuel boosters as it climbed, the three main engines burning steadily all the while. Then they, too, were finally silent and they had reached orbit, the first step.

The deltoid spacecraft drifted for forty-five minutes as the crew prepared to make the orbital shift to align with the NavSynch 7 satellite still thousands of miles above them. The Shuttle itself could never reach the necessary altitude, but its payload—the smaller, remotely operated space bus and the antenna array it would carry to NavSynch 7—could. First, however, they had to refine their orbit. This was accomplished with a single long burn a little less than one hour after lift-off, which was further refined by two minor corrections.

Then the on-board mission specialist from Hughes, who was charged with controlling the space bus, went to work at her console at the rear of the Shuttle's flight deck, opening the huge doors that began a few feet behind the flight deck itself, and which formed two-thirds of the length of the Space Shuttle. The unpressurized cargo bay, which contained the space bus and its payload, was now open to the void. The specialist worked the controls that released the bus and its payload from the barnlike confines of the Shuttle's cargo bay, springing it free of the Shuttle.

The Shuttle pilots then began carefully maneuvering clear of the unmanned space bus, the sound of the Shuttle's maneuvering thrusters heard clearly in their pressurized cabin. The mission specialist looked on from her post behind the pilots as they drifted to a position some four miles from the space bus. The final countdown for the remotely controlled bus then fell to the mission specialist, her voice running systematically through the final items.

The Shuttle pilots watched as the bus's engine ignited, pushing the payload steadily outward, away from them, climbing for a higher orbit, synchronous with NavSynch 7 high over the Pacific. Then the silent flare of the rocket engine was gone, lost in the background of stars.

Auslander had long since concluded that there was no way out. He had known there was no way out when the Joint Chiefs had first descended on him with the ASAT question. He had known there was no way out when he became enmeshed in the *Adresteia* conspiracy. He sure as hell knew there was no way out now that it had all come apart around him. Still, he had to admit that it was interesting.

As Secretary of Defense, just what was he supposed to do, anyway? There were those damn ASATs out there somewhere in the Siberian wastes, as if they were some personal curse meant to hound him to his death.

Impassive, implacable, one of those utterly inescapable facts which are more than maddening.

Who would have imagined, from seeing the man that day in Shaw's office when they had given him his orders, that d'Alembert would prove capable of something like this? He was a man off his guard then. Able, he supposed, but hardly worthy of inspiring outright fear. He inspired a certain quotient of fear now. Of course, the fact that he had something over two hundred fifty nuclear warheads under his direct personal command had something to do with that.

Not that they were aimed at Auslander alone.

He liked Devlin. He was a good deal more forthright than the others. Which, in turn, made his assessment that much less welcome. One chance in ten, he had said, of stopping d'Alembert. Ten chances to one of his stopping them. He did not like the odds.

D'Alembert would win this one, if it could be called winning. At any rate, as far as he was concerned, he would at least stop them. Mann wouldn't find any other way of dealing with those sites, and he knew it. They all knew it. Let him try. He would fail. Then, perhaps, he would turn his full attention to this, their more immediate problem.

If word of this . . . *mess* ever got to Elliott he would skin their hides. Personally. He knew about Elliott's temper when he let it loose—which was, thank the good Lord, not often.

So they were dependent, horribly dependent, on security—Collier. Collier could at times be plodding and profane in an Army sort of way, but he was reasonably competent. Certainly not incompetent. There was some slight measure of hope.

Mann, on the other hand, was too competent—too

competently capable of inserting himself in matters he ought not to be involved in. Oh, hell, how could it be otherwise? He had left gaps and Mann had filled them. That was natural enough. Nature may not really care one way or the other about a vacuum, but power abhors one with a vengeance. Seizes it.

Shaw seemed to him to be in a peculiar variety of professional shock. In several ways he thought him to be the best of the three, but he felt that Shaw had been frustrated in dealing with Mann—and it was his man, Shaw's man, a Navy man—even if a submariner—who had turned against them. Shaw might bear a sympathy.

CIA—and NSA, even more—worried him. They were bureaucratic terra incognita. CIA was reasonably certain, he thought. They had been burned before, though. NSA was hale and hearty. In a position to know, electronically, nearly anything. NSA was the black heart and mind of the intelligence beast, the dark silences that were the core memory of some cosmic Central Processing Unit.

Well, he couldn't convince Mann and the rest that d'Alembert had, in fact, stopped them cold the minute he sent that message—not until they were ready to be convinced. They'd begun that process. Hopefully, he thought, they would see it for themselves soon, accept it as he had—as fact. Hopefully, too, they would see it soon.

In any case, there was nothing he could do. It was out of his hands.

Aboard *Adresteia*, Fox had the con. Thomson, the weapons officer, passed the time with him.

"Is the captain taking the con when we make next contact?" he asked.

"I think so. Why?"

"Just wondering."

Thomson seemed hesitant.

"Something bothering you?" Fox asked him.

"Just the usual. What you'd expect."

Fox nodded sympathetically.

"What do you think they're going to do next?" Thomson asked.

"I'd think," Fox answered, "that that's probably what they're asking themselves about us at this point. Of course, we have no more way of knowing that than they do of knowing about us."

Stewart entered the control room from the corridor leading aft.

"Are you two chattering like old women again?" he asked in greeting.

Thomson smiled to himself. "I guess so," he said.

"Well, cut it out," Stewart said. "It makes me nervous. An old man like me doesn't like to be made nervous."

"An old man?" Fox asked.

"At the rate you're jabbering," Stewart said, "I'm going to be old and gray from listening to the two of you. Thomson, haven't you anything better to do with your time? I'm planning on a little friendly poker and you're invited."

"You're on, 'old man.'"

"Good. I can always use some extra money."

"He only gives checks," Fox put in.

"Long as they don't bounce," Stewart answered.

The two men started from the control room, Thomson heading down the ladder first. As Stewart started down after him he glanced back at Fox. Fox silently mouthed the word "thanks" at him. Stewart shrugged that it was nothing.

"All right, graybeard, cut the deck," sounded from below.

Stewart mocked an old man's voice. "Don't be too quick to be shorn, you young whippersnapper."

Fox was alone again with the helmsmen, the sonar man, the others. With *Adresteia* and the ocean she moved in.

Orcus ran like one of the Furies. Bent on exacting vengeance. Redressing the balance. Some laws could not be broken. She ran hard, with everything she had, making a speed that was officially listed only as "in excess of forty knots" and which was *considerably* in excess of forty knots. Her narrow-beam sonar scanned the ice above and the bottom below, each of which still allowed her ample margin.

With the orders, Hansen had changed. He had told no one, would tell no one till it was time. But *he* knew. The Strait was still before them. Hansen had attempted passage in last winter's freakishly severe conditions and had failed. This winter was reported worse. It might be the climate was shifting, or it might be a vital shift in currents or ice balance, but whatever it was, it was a problem. *Orcus* was no icebreaker, strong though her alloy steel hull was against the pressure of the depths.

D'Alembert had been his mentor, his friend. Now he was a betrayer or a madman, but Hansen did not know why, could not imagine why, though he had tried for all the hours since they had gotten under way.

With the hours that *Orcus* spent in driving on toward the Bering Strait, the Strait and d'Alembert and *Adresteia* began a slow fusion in Hansen's mind: obstacles.

"Helm, give me one three zero meters, steady as she goes."

Hansen had not yet become just a mask, but the process had begun. He was faced with orders. He had dedicated his life to his country and the service. He would face those orders and he would face the obstacles. He would drive *Orcus* on. They were within a few hours of the currents that marked the outermost approaches to the strait.

He would see them through.

"Mal, Collier here."

"Yes, Mike?"

"I just got off the horn with CIA. About that inquiry you wanted to make . . . ? Forget it. They can't do anything for us with the ASATs."

"Or won't."

"That, too,"

"Shit, Mike. That leaves us completely out in the cold."

"That's the way I figure it."

"Shaw and I couldn't come up with a thing."

"Did you really figure you would?"

"No. Not really. Damn it! You sure CIA is tight?"

"They won't come up from behind us. They're in with us to that extent."

"I know. I know."

"It's not that they're unsympathetic, Mal; they just aren't willing to hang their ass out the window and see if anyone wants to kick it or not."

"A bunch of real patriots—sitting behind their desks, getting fat."

"I think that's about the picture, Mal."

"Don't worry. I've got the picture."

President Elliott had briefed his two senior advisers on the information Auslander had furnished him. Neither of them was pleased. They were, in fact, more alarmed than Elliott that the Joint Chiefs had been concealing the existence of the ASATs from him thus far. Elliott, however, was not surprised. He had been dealing with the Joint Chiefs for a while. It had not surprised him in the least that they considered it their prerogative to change missile assignments and provide a commander with special priority orders in event of war—all without consulting the Commander in Chief. Nor did it surprise him that they wanted to formulate their position on the matter faultlessly before letting him even know the threat existed.

It hadn't completely astonished the other two men either, but it did alarm them. Eliott wondered for a moment if he might be missing something. He didn't like that idea.

The night passed. Devlin was up early, smoking a pipe and reading the papers when the phone rang.

"Quent? Jean. Remember me?"

"I remember you, all right, Worthington."

"There's no way that sounds like a compliment," Worthington said.

"For a woman of your mature years, you are remarkably perceptive," Devlin replied coldly.

"My years are no more mature than yours, Devlin. Neither of us will see forty again, and that's not why I called."

"That provides some measure of reassurance."

"This is strictly business, Devlin. I have something I want to ask you about."

"Listen, Jean, I really have other things to do. Why don't you just phone my press office or lurk around a few dark corridors—whatever you usually do."

There was a frustrated sigh on Worthington's end of the line.

"Have it your way, Quent. I thought we were still friends, even if we've had our differences. I just wanted to inquire about a submarine commander of yours. If you want me to forget it, I'll forget it."

"Forget it."

"Okay. Consider it done."

For a variety of reasons, Devlin quickly reconsidered.

"Just a second, Jean. Maybe I can help you. What's his name?"

"D'Alembert. Alexander d'Alembert."

CHAPTER 14

With all the momentum of her seventeen thousand tons *Adresteia* neared the surface, prepared again to contend with the Joint Chiefs.

With all the momentum of his commitment, his determination, d'Alembert held the con, held them steady, his officers at his side.

"Communications, make the link."

"Aye, aye, sir," the operator said. Then, "Skipper, there's a voice channel open to us this time."

D'Alembert considered the implications of this new development. He turned to Fox. Fox's expression was noncommittal.

"Gentlemen," d'Alembert said, "I want absolute silence during this exchange."

The order was understood. D'Alembert lifted the microphone, said, "Patch it through."

A few moments later Mann's voice filled *Adresteia*'s control room.

"Good day, Captain. I thought our understanding of one another might improve if we were able to speak in a more human fashion."

"General Mann, I presume," d'Alembert said.

"You presume a great deal, Captain—but in this case, at least, you presume correctly."

"Are the others there?" d'Aembert asked.

"They are."

"Then we may proceed."

"We may, Captain. What may I do for you?"

D'Alembert took a breath, keyed the microphone to life.

"I want your final decision this time, gentlemen."

"I would think, d'Alembert, that our final decision is apparent in the very fact of this conversation."

"This communication raises more than one possibility in my mind, General."

There was a brief silence before Mann replied, the laser-borne voice as free of static as ever.

"First, Captain, I need to know how long you will give us to arrange for the transfer of the money."

"Until the first of the year. Midnight GMT."

Again a pause, while Mann presumably conferred with his fellows.

"Accepted."

There were expressions of relief in the control room at that single word.

"I would feel more at ease, General, if I heard the same from the other principals."

There was the sound of the microphone being shifted.

"This is General Collier, d'Alembert. You win."

Then the next.

"Shaw, d'Alembert. We'll give you your point."

Then the next.

"This is Secretary of Defense Auslander speaking, Captain. I want this matter ended as quickly and as gracefully as we can manage—you have my word on that."

"Then I thank you, Mr. Secretary," d'Alembert answered with steel in his voice.

Mann recaptured the microphone.

"Just so that there are no misunderstandings, d'Alembert, this is my understanding of our agreement. You will take no action and return to your base. We will transfer twenty-five million to your Swiss account before you do so. When you return to base we will arrange an explanation that your patrol was ended ahead of schedule for technical considerations, and we will arrange for an adequate explanation of the early retirement and/or reassignment of you and whatever of your senior officers are necessary—just to keep the record straight. You will, of course, be free to do what you choose so long as you maintain absolute secrecy about our role in this affair for the rest of your lives."

"The ASATs?" d'Alembert asked.

"We will take no action. Auslander will bring the President up to date while leaving this incident out of the matter."

"I have a number of junior officers and control room crew whose cover 'retirement' will also have to be arranged if you want to protect yourselves."

Mann was not pleased at this thought.

"We'll manage to work something out—contamination, perhaps."

"Sounds appropriate."

"Are we straight, then, d'Alembert?"

"As straight as we're going to get, General."

Mann ignored this.

"I'll need several days to arrange the details," he said. "You'll have to lie low until then. Do you have any problems with that?"

"We'll live with it."

"Good." Mann hesitated. "I'm not going to apologize to you, d'Alembert—I respect your intelligence too much for that. But I do regret this—and I expect you realize there was no malevolence involved here."

D'Alembert tried not to sound bitter.

"Of course not. It was all in the roll of the dice. Nothing personal."

"I do have an additional requirement of you, Captain. I'll need you to make periodic contact with us—however brief—to assure me that everything is in good order. Once every twenty-four hours."

D'Alembert became more wary.

"Let's make it every thirty-six hours, General, and I will indeed be brief."

A slight edge glinted in Mann's voice.

"Accepted."

D'Alembert snapped the microphone back to life. "Gentlemen, I will expect you to transfer the funds to my wife in Zurich—I'm sure you know all about that by now."

"We know," answered Mann's disembodied voice.

His men's eyes were on d'Alembert. The Joint Chiefs had agreed. There was nothing more to say.

"*Adresteia* out," he said.

The tension hung heavy in the control room. They had learned, it seemed, that they had succeeded. Yet there were no certitudes sensed in that steeled space.

"Take her down, helm."

As they spoke, the Air Force Space Shuttle drifted serenely in its steady, circular orbit, the on-board mission specialist hard at work at her remote control station at the rear of the Shuttle's flight deck. The small, remotely operated space bus that she controlled had lifted the necessary antenna arrays and their data processing package to the high orbiting satellite. NavSynch 7 was now clearly visible to the specialist through the cameras mounted on the space bus. She studied this telemetered picture and the accompanying data, guiding the bus's final approach to the communications satellite, then turning to the work of guiding the robot vehicle's manipulator arms to make the necessary connections with NavSynch 7's existing data links.

It was difficult work, directing the movements of mechanical arms thousands of miles away. Slow. The specialist that Hughes had provided was capable enough, but this was a hastily planned mission. She was soon enmeshed in a number of unanticipated hang-ups, and the timetable for completion began its inexorable slippage as she conferred with the Shuttle crew beside her and the technical advisers on the ground. It would be done, but it would take time.

Mann drummed his fingers rhythmically on the table-top.

"What's the final verdict from CIA?" Auslander asked Collier.

"They'll maintain surveillance on the wife," Collier said, "but that's all. There's nothing they can do to help us. We're on our own from here on out."

"I thought there was supposed to be support for this mission," Auslander said with annoyance.

"There was," Collier said. "They would have liked us to succeed—but they won't put their heads into the meatgrinder for us."

"We're in the cold, cruel world," Shaw said to Auslander.

"As far as they're concerned, that's about the picture," Collier observed. "Other than that, though, security is in good order. I haven't many people to work with, but we can contain it."

Mann continued to drum his fingers on the table-top.

Shaw addressed himself to their shared silence. "*Orcus* should be nearing the Bering Strait," he said. "She probably won't be able to establish communications with command until she's either succeeded or failed. In any case, not for some time. I've been coordinating what routine antisubmarine warfare exercises we have ongoing in the Pacific with Devlin so that if anyone picks up *Adresteia* by blind luck, we'll know about it—fast."

Mann, still preoccupied, drummed his fingers.

"Mal?" Shaw asked him.

Mann spoke as if he were only half there.

"The Shuttle is working. It'll have time. There are minor hitches in the interface that have to be worked around by the softwave people. Twenty to twenty-two hours is the current estimate."

Mann's mind, in fact, waited now on a single entity and their shared fate—*Orcus*. Hansen must reach the Pacific. *Must.*

"What level of resolution do you expect?" Shaw asked him.

Must.

"The current figures are four-hundred-eighty-mile radius with a point five factor," Mann answered.

Must.

"That's not going to help all that much," Shaw said.

"I know that," Mann said sharply. "But it will help. It will narrow it down. It's *something*."

Auslander cleared his throat for attention.

"I can probably hold Elliott off for a week if I have to," he said.

"That reminds me," Shaw said. "We've got a problem with Devlin beyond the hundred-twenty-hour mark."

"Yeah, I know," Collier said.

"Let's not worry about that yet," Mann said. "It's too far off at this point."

Auslander seized the conversation again.

"But I don't want to go that route," he said.

"What?" someone said.

"We're just digging ourselves in deeper," Auslander persisted. "The consensus is that we have, at best, one chance in ten of sinking *Adresteia*. At best."

"It is a chance," Shaw said determinedly.

"And it's a chance that can go to hell in a handbasket," Auslander snapped back. "Just as the chance of giving d'Alembert this mission went to hell. I think we should seriously consider cutting our losses."

Mann was no longer preoccupied.

"What the fuck is that supposed to mean, Auslander?"

"That means I think we're acting like fools. That we're running scared."

"Speak for yourself," Shaw said angrily.

"Don't give me that crap," Auslander said as coolly as he could manage. "The point here is that at this point we're only in just so deep. We gave d'Alembert the orders. We shouldn't have—but we did. And it went wrong. If we go to the President at this point, in a united front, that's all there is to it."

"That's *all?*" Mann demanded. "That's *all?* I don't believe this, Auslander."

Auslander tried not to react. "Listen to me and listen to me well, gentlemen. We are now steadily becoming committed to the attempted destruction of an American submarine and her crew. If *that* goes wrong in any way . . ."

There was a silence. Everyone understood Auslander's argument. No one wanted to listen to it.

"What, specifically, are you suggesting?" Mann asked.

"One way or the other, we've been stopped," Auslander said in as reasonable a tone as he could summon. "There is no way we can take out those ASATs now. Which, I'd like to point out, was the point of this whole exercise."

"I don't think we need you to tell us that, Mr. Secretary," Collier opined. "I don't think we've forgotten it."

"I sure haven't," Shaw said.

"I'm not suggesting anyone has," Auslander resumed his argument. "My point is simply that we're now committed to nothing more important than saving our own skins. It's better to just minimize our losses. Face the music."

Mann was livid.

"It is not a matter of 'saving our skins,' Mr. Secretary. Or of facing the music. If we have to saunter up to the President of the United States and confess our sins and errors like bad little children we don't simply lose a little face. What kind of naif are you, anyway, Auslander?"

Auslander protested.

Mann out-shouted him.

"Just one minute. Hear me out, Mr. Secretary. We started this thing, and we're going to finish it—one way or the other. The military leadership in this country is eternally accused of a lack of competence. Any politician who can't balance his own checkbook thinks he's the expert and we don't know our ass from our elbow."

Mann paused for half an instant, settling into it.

"Now some of that has been our own fault—and a hell of a lot more has been dumped on us for various political reasons. We undertook this mission, Mr. Secretary, for the simple reason that we felt it was the only sure way to assure the country's safety. It would be a fundamental mistake to have that decision perceived as an error."

Mann glared at Auslander, though his voice was level now.

"How will that affect the relationship between civilian and military leadership—when our judgment matters? And how many more lives could that cost in the long run?"

"I didn't mean to imply . . ." Auslander trailed off into silence.

"The point here, Auslander, is not that we're trying to save ourselves—which we are. The point is that we're right. We have not been taken seriously enough at times in the past, and there have been consequences. We're not trying to save ourselves, Mr. Secretary, we're trying to do our job. To save our country."

There was an audible silence when Mann finished speaking. Auslander stared down into his reflection in the polished tabletop.

"Let's get on with it, then," he said weakly.

Orcus no longer made flank speed. She moved now at a walking pace, confined by a shallow bottom, packed ice above her, restricted waters. They had reached the Bering Strait.

The tac/nav situation display presented a detailed representation of their sonar readings integrated with a navigational display. Their sonar ranged actively now, emitting pulsed sounds in shifting directions, the echoes awaited and analyzed by the computers, the laser range-finding gear standing by for detailed scanning.

"Looks bad," Coppi said.

"Yes," Hansen answered, engrossed in the details of the display.

"Do you want to come at it from a different approach?" Coppi asked his captain.

"No, Angel. Not yet."

"Okay, Skipper."

Orcus was a grimly serious place. It was very quiet, exceedingly businesslike. A hush had begun to grow as they neared the Strait. The men sensed Hansen's determination, though they could not know the reason for it. They had begun to share in it. *Orcus* would not fail. They would not be stopped.

The Soviet vessel had shadowed *Orcus* from the first, though it had fallen far behind. *Orcus* had outclassed them, outrun them by an incredible margin—but her course had become clear before they had lost her.

So the Soviets, too, made for the Bering Strait, silently stalking *Orcus* in a turn of the game.

They were still somewhat distant, but they ran steadily onward, closing the gap. With time, they would be there.

Devlin parked his car outside the nondescript Howard Johnson's where he and Worthington had agreed to meet. She was waiting inside.

He ordered coffee and took a seat at her table.

"What's this about one of my submarine commanders, Worthington?" he asked.

All business, she thought.

"Just a rumor I'm checking out," she said, stirring her tea.

Devlin made a considerable effort to appear utterly unfazed.

"A rumor?"

"More or less," she said. "I need background."

"If you want background, the press office could give you what you need," Devlin said.

"I need an insider."

"Like the last time?"

Worthington brushed her hair out of her eyes, lifted her cup.

"I told you before, Quenten, that I developed another inside contact on the procurement scandal. I didn't violate your confidence in any way."

"You won't mind if I'm a little doubtful of that."

"As a matter of fact, I do."

Devlin shrugged.

"D'Alembert?" she pursued.

"He's a captain. Gold crew, SSBN *Adresteia*. A Trident boat, *Mjollnir* class. He's young yet. He'll go far."

"Anything else?"

"A wife. A couple of children. No pets that I know of."

"You're right," she said. "I could have gotten that from the press office."

"Not the part about the pets," he said.

Devlin, who had chosen to confine the inquiry, chose to become more serious.

"What have you got, Jean?"

Worthington sighed.

"Suppose d'Alembert were the object of an internal security check run at CIA? Very careful. Very hasty. Very irregular."

"When?" Devlin asked, noncommittal.

"Concluded on the ninth. Do you know anything about it?"

"No," Devlin answered truthfully. "I don't. But why so much commotion?"

"Is it every day, Quent, that CIA suddenly develops an obsessive interest in one of your submarine commanders? And his officers?"

"His officers?"

"Yes."

Devlin thought about this. What bothered him was the date. The ninth? That was impossibly early. Mann had mentioned that d'Alembert had been briefed within forty-eight hours of their first hearing of the ASATs. He remembered that distinctly.

The ninth?

"Okay, Jean, you've got my interest. I'll check it out."

"Thanks."

"Look, Jean, don't kid yourself. I consider d'Alembert a good officer with a future. I don't want to see him ruined by some unconfirmed internal suspicions that I don't even know about. Or any cheap journalistic angles."

"Thanks again," she said, her voice bound in irony.

"Just so we understand one another."

"We understand one another, Devlin."

"Then that's clear."

"Perfectly."

"Then I'll be going," Devlin said, getting up. "I'll get back to you."

"Okay."

Devlin left the room with no further words exchanged, leaving Worthington alone with the plastic-veneered table and her cold cup of tea.

CHAPTER 15

D'Alembert and Fox had been meeting for some time in the privacy of d'Alembert's cabin following their communication with Auslander and the Joint Chiefs.

"I don't trust them, Alex," Fox said.

"Neither do I," d'Alembert answered him. "But they've agreed to our conditions, so what more can we do?"

"I don't know. Except to keep our heads up."

D'Alembert looked at his watch.

"Time for the wardroom session."

The two men left, made their way to the wardroom where Stewart, Thomson, and Michaels waited. They took their places.

"Uh, Captain?" Stewart asked.

"Yes?"

"We were talking while we were waiting for you and I just thought we should tell you that we all feel that we're a little nervous about General Mann."

"I'm a little nervous, too, Mr. Stewart," the captain said, "so you have company. Do any of you have any definite suggestions?"

"No, Skipper," Michaels said. "We just don't feel we can trust them—not that we have too much of a choice."

"That's the problem," Fox said. "We can't launch on the North Slope because we don't trust them in some vague and undefined sense."

"That's the problem, all right," Thomson said.

"Mr. Fox and I have been giving this some thought, too," d'Alembert said, "and, while we certainly can't anticipate every possible eventuality, we still believe we have an acceptable chance—regardless of Mann's or anyone else's questionable faith—once we can get ourselves established ashore with that money to buy some security. I don't believe they'll risk certain exposure. But I do want us to be prepared for any eventuality we can anticipate, which is why I've called this session. I want everyone to feel free to throw out anything they can think of, no matter how wild, for discussion—to see if there's anything we're overlooking. First, though, I want to ask if there are any second thoughts. Are there?"

He looked at them.

"None? Good. One word of caution, then. If anything in any way unusual happens while anyone other than myself has the con, I want to be alerted instantly. And I do mean instantly—without hesitation. Even the least aberration. Is that understood?"

It was.

"Captain?" Thomson asked.

"Yes."

"Well, Captain, I've been wondering. If Mann can't be trusted, perhaps we should force a showdown— demand that he tell the President everything and have the President call us on the executive command channel. That would be a foolproof mark of authenticity."

"Michaels, are you still certain of that?"

"Yes, Skipper. I've studied it carefully. We couldn't be certain from our end if we were being shunted aside if we were to initiate a communication to the President over the channels open to us. But there's no way to fake a message we receive on the executive command channel."

D'Alembert rethought the question one more time.

"No," he said. "It occurred to me a long time ago to try that approach. But it would force the Joint Chiefs to face Elliott. If they were willing to do that, they wouldn't be in the bind they're in now—and neither would we. It's their fear of exposure—chiefly to the President—that's the one thing we have really going for us. We have to leave them a way out."

Fox nodded, then the others. It had seemed a hope for only a moment.

A disappointed silence began to fall. D'Alembert faced it.

"My question is this: If they are foolish enough to lay a trap for us, what will it look like?"

Ice above. The floor of the ocean rose. *Orcus* pushed on.

"Ten meters beneath the keel, Skipper."

"All stop."

"Aye, aye, sir. All stop."

Hansen studied the tac/nav, considered their position.

"Ahead dead slow, come fifteen degrees to port."

The orders were verified. *Orcus* altered course slightly.

"Jesus, Skipper, do you really expect to get us through this stuff?" Coppi asked.

"It's possible, Angel," Hansen answered.

"Maybe for an icebreaker."

Both men watched the readings as the bottom rose to meet them.

"Full reverse!" Hansen called out.

Coppi relaxed for an instant as their propeller took hold. He wondered why it was so important that they reach the Pacific. Hansen had told no one. And he was taking chances.

The hours of probing for a path passed slowly, with no success. Coppi relieved an exhausted Hansen, *Orcus* inching cautiously onward beneath the ice.

This was suicide, Coppi thought. He pushed them on.

It was Mann that Devlin phoned first when he returned to his office.

"How's the NavSynch modification coming, Mal?" he asked him.

"Slow," Mann answered. "But it's coming."

"Good. I need all the help I can get. I haven't heard from *Orcus*, but that's no surprise. She must still be at it."

"Let me know the minute you hear anything."

"Sure thing. Also, I wanted to make sure I had my timeline straight on everything, so that if anything comes up, I can cover. When did the CNO and Auslander brief d'Alembert?"

"The fifteenth," Mann said.

"Okay," Devlin said, then continued on into a few other housekeeping details so that Mann wouldn't suspect anything.

Finally, it seemed, he was able to hang up. He stared at the wall for a while, making sure.

Worthington said she had it on good authority that

the security check was completed by the ninth. Mann had said from the first that there had been little time from the discovery of the ASATs to d'Alembert's briefing—no more than forty-eight hours. That they had had to act in haste. Devlin thought it all over for a while, still making sure in his mind. Then he was sure.

Mann had lied.

The session aboard *Adresteia* was winding down, the officers showing signs of their deep fatigue from the strain of the last few days. D'Alembert didn't want to push them too hard. They had to pace themselves. To go the distance.

"Okay," he said. "None of us believe that there's any way for them to mount an effective operation of any magnitude against us without blowing their cover and word reaching the President. So that rules that out. If they're looking to trap us they'll have channeled routine operating ASW reports to the CNO. So we need to be cautious. It's a big ocean. If they don't know where to start looking, no single vessel can hope to find us, and one or two vessels is all they can risk. Also, once we've got someone safely ashore for additional insurance, we'll be that much better off. Charles, what's the most recent estimate of our running time to the transfer point?"

"Forty-seven hours, Captain."

"Let's reduce speed to one-third, then. We can afford the delay, I think, and it's a better compromise. Any other questions?"

There were none.

"Very well, then, gentlemen, let's take it nice and easy. I don't want so much as an amorous whale to notice this boat."

* * *

Devlin picked up the phone, punched out the number, waited for the answering voice.

"Jean?"

"Yes?"

"Devlin."

"I know *that*."

Devlin was in a hurry. He sensed time might prove to be in short supply.

"Jean, you're right. Something is funny. I want to warn you to keep a very low profile on this, whatever it is, while I look into it. I'll get back to you."

"All right, Quent, I'll keep it quiet."

"Please do," Devlin said. "I don't want to sound melodramatic, but your life might depend on it."

"Jesus, what is this?"

"I don't know yet. When I do I'll get back to you."

Devlin hung up. Dialed again.

He couldn't work through channels, not with the Joint Chiefs engaged in an effort to deceive him. He had, fortunately, a friend at NSA, a young man who was tied into everything that happened in half of NSA's operations, their ranking computer expert. He was worth a try.

So he called Kenneth Jamison.

D'Alembert lay supine in the dark on his bunk, courting sleep. He was emotionally and physically near exhaustion. He was the captain. He was in command. Must not hesitate, must not doubt. . . .

He had to clear his mind, rest. Involuntarily he thought of Morgan and Jennifer and Joshua in Switzerland—then reminded himself it was better not to think of it. He tried to focus his mind on the sound and the tempo of his own breathing, force himself to sleep. He could not.

Surrounded by the enormous strength of *Adresteia's* alloy hull, enclosed by the darkness of the sea and of that arced steel that protected him from the sea, d'Alembert did his best to forget everything, to hear only the measured silence that stole into the space between breaths.

President Elliott had phoned and told Secretary Auslander to report to the Oval Office. Auslander had done so. The President told him to have a seat, offered him a drink. It was late in the day and Auslander asked for bourbon, which the President's secretary furnished for him. Elliott drank nothing.

"What's happening with the Joint Chiefs?" the President asked the Secretary of Defense.

"The same, Mr. President."

"No change?"

Auslander took a drink.

"None."

"Well, when do you think they're going to get around to advising the President of this present danger, Bill? Aren't they taking their own sweet time about this?"

Auslander sipped warily at his drink.

"You know the Joint Chiefs, Mr. President."

Elliott, Auslander noted, seemed annoyed. Perhaps ominously annoyed.

"Do they still have this submarine commander on special alert?" the President asked him.

"Yes. They do."

"Any other precautions?"

"They're trying to arrange alternate lines of communication and control so they'll have an effective alternative if the Soviets were to take out the command net with the ASATs."

Elliott paced the room.

"How long will that take?"

"I'd guess a week, maybe two, for anything at all effective."

The conversation continued, Elliott pressing Auslander for more information on the activities of the Joint Chiefs over the last few days. Auslander poured himself another drink, doing his level best to appear only as distressed as he should appear. It proved, for him, to be an unbearably difficult conversation—more of an inquisition. Did Elliott know something? He finished the drink. If Elliott did know something . . .

Auslander took one more drink, decided to take the gamble.

"Christ, Mr. President," he interrupted.

"Yes . . . ?"

"Something's gone crazy with that submarine commander, Mr. President. He's taken the whole thing into his own hands. The Chiefs are trying to stop him. They begged me to keep quiet until they had a chance. But . . ."

Elliott became almost eerily soft-spoken.

"He what?"

Auslander's mind raced ahead at maximum effort. He was as sober as he had ever been. Why should he just go down with the Joint Chiefs, damn it, when he could pull them out of the whole thing? He could work it out.

"Mr. President," he said, "we received a message a short time ago warning us that this captain, d'Alembert, had decided to launch on the ASAT installations on the first of the year—warning us that we should be prepared to handle any possible Soviet reaction."

Auslander waited anxiously for a sign of Elliott's re-action—any sign. There was none. Elliott continued to slowly pace the carpeted floor of the Oval Office.

"Okay, Bill, let's talk," the President said.

Orcus shuddered with the impact, as did her executive officer. He looked at Hansen.

"We're wedged, Skipper," he said, confirming the fact.

"Engineering, give me your stress figures," Hansen called out. The figures appeared on the tac/nav.

Hansen winced.

"Sonar, direct a laser sweep forward, put the image up. I want detail."

The results of the scan appeared on the display, an analysis of what could be learned of the ice that wedged them solid. It was a marginal situation in any of a number of ways. *Orcus* was rigged for collision, her watertight doors firmly secured. Hansen studied the information as the hull protested audibly from the strain.

"Angel?" he asked.

"Maybe, Skipper. Maybe not. It's risky."

"We'll go for it," Hansen decided. "Engineering, I'm going to need your maximum effort. Everything you can give me brought up as quickly as possible. Got that?"

"Aye, aye, Skipper."

"Helm, I'm going to leave control discretion to you. Steer for minimum resistance. Minimize your deflections as well as you can. Got that?"

"Got it, Skipper."

They were ready for the final attempt.

"Engineering, give me everything you've got. Now."

Orcus threw herself against the unyielding ice. The cry of the tortured hull against the ice echoed through the spaces of the boat, promising failure and death beneath the ice.

Hansen clenched a fist.

"Through, damn it, *through!*"

The strain readings rose in great ragged jumps as the propeller took hold, pushed them hard.

Then with a great rush and a last cry of the protesting ice, they were through.

Orcus had left the Arctic Ocean.

Found her way to the Pacific.

CHAPTER 16

The sun struck the Space Shuttle's wings as its low orbit drifted it again into daylight. Their mission was
nearing completion. The remotely operated space bus
controlled by the mission specialist had made the necessary connections between the original NavSynch 7
military communications satellite and the new antenna array with its data-processing package. What remained were the systems checks.

Finally, both the mission specialist and the ground
operators were satisfied. The specialist left the job of
retrieving the space bus to the Shuttle's crew, headed
below for some rest.

Several hours later, the bus was securely stowed in
the cargo bay, the doors that formed the Shuttle's
spine were secured. The pilots completed the final maneuvers for the reentry burn, firing the main engines
to brake them from orbit, maneuvering again to proper reentry attitude.

The Shuttle made first contact with the upper
atmosphere with its nose pitched high, taking the heat
on the ceramic tiles that lined its underbelly, beginning the long gliding descent that would carry their
flaming reentry the length of the Pacific—the long
glide for California and home.

The aide entered.

"Shuttle's landed, **General**."

"Good. Seven operational?"

"On the numbers, sir."

"Good."

Mann had his localization capablity. When *Adresteia* next linked with NavSynch7 her laser beam would no longer suffice to mask her location. The beam would be carefully scanned, the data coded and relayed to the command center for processing. The data would be very crude, but it would exist.

For the first time, Mann knew, he had a solid chance. *Orcus* was in the Bering Sea—had made the Pacific. NavSynch 7 would tell them where to begin the search for *Adresteia*. Then it would be up to Hansen, who knew d'Alembert best.

Orcus had lost a great deal of time in seeking out—and finally forcing—a passage to the Pacific. When the nameless Soviet submarine that shadowed her reached her tail in the Bering Strait, the trail was cool—but not cold. Shkodin, the Soviet commander, knew the Arctic and the ever-shifting ice well. *Orcus* had opened the way for them. The Russians, too, were soon in the Pacific, gaining time on the American submarine that had so aroused their professional curiosity.

They had gained time, a great deal of time—but not enough to overtake *Orcus*. They were a missile submarine, and one inferior to the latest American technology. *Orcus* had a lead. Even if she continued to make high speed, making in the process as much disturbance as she ever would, the trail would be hard to follow.

Shkodin had his work cut out for him. But he was an old hand, and his superiors had been more than merely intrigued by his report of *Orcus*'s unheard-of behavior. He had his orders and they were not opposed to his natural bent—or his enthusiasm for turning the tables.

Shkodin would see what he could do.

Adresteia proceeded on course with extraordinary precaution, even for a missile submarine. Their speed was fairly low. They ran at depths near their operating limits. The sonar watch was extremely sharp.

The greater part of the crew, who knew nothing of the events that had, in fact, determined their lives for the last several days, continued to know nothing. Their duties were the same as always. They knew *Adresteia* was engaged in some form of extraordinary secret exercise, but this was by no means entirely unheard of. It was better for them, d'Alembert had decided from the first, not to know—and they would not.

The control room crew, however, and the officers, knew their peril all too well. The concession made by the Joint Chiefs had provided only slight reassurance. Fear still ruled, well reined though it was. The fear, the tension it produced, was a form of challenge. They were submariners, volunteers, highly trained, and they were d'Alembert's crew. They were proud, and they would handle any challenge that presented itself to them. This evasive form of challenge—a variety of the waiting game—was the most difficult, but it was by no means new to them. It was essentially a variant of their normal patrol routine—to leave port, submerge,

187

avoid any form of detection for the length of the patrol, then, finally, surface again and return home. A tedious and a difficult business. They could handle it.

And if the form suddenly shifted in shape, required an active response . . . they would handle that, too—without hesitation.

D'Alembert knew this, knew it well, holding in his mind the key word that would fully arm their weapons at a moment's notice. *Adresteia* was one, a single entity, a force beneath the sea, an aspect of waiting death for any that might oppose her. D'Alembert held that force in check, governed it. He would do his utmost to avoid the need of unleashing it. Still, it was there. Waiting.

They sailed on.

Spencer Elliott heard Auslander through. The Secretary had retreated—whatever his reasons—to the line intended earlier by the Joint Chiefs before it had all gone wrong—that d'Alembert had been briefed, but was acting on his own. The tale Auslander presented Elliott mirrored that original intention perfectly, inappropriate as that mirroring would now seem to Mann and the others.

Elliott, having heard him out, made no gesture toward indecision. The minute Auslander had been dismissed from his office he was on the phone from the Oval Office. He wanted Mann and he wanted him fast. Alone.

Elliott gave Mann no clue to the reason for his sudden summons to the White House, said simply to be there quickly. He would let Mann wonder for a while.

* * *

Adresteia moved slowly toward the surface, extended her sensor and communications arrays, directed her laser carrier beam toward NavSynch 7.

D'Alembert was unwilling to linger near the surface, so he simply transmitted in a single pulse the coded message assuring the Joint Chiefs of *Adresteia*'s continued reality, then gave the orders that would return them to their maximum operating depth above the deep basins of the Pacific.

The link-time with NavSynch 7 was short, measured in microseconds, and the antenna array was crude, hastily cobbled together. The laser beam was well defined, solidly on target as it reached NavSynch 7, leaving little directional information for the processors newly installed aboard the high-orbiting satellite. The first data transmitted to the Joint Chiefs, therefore, was crude stuff—but it was the first, and gained in significance from that fact.

Within minutes of *Adresteia*'s transmission to the relay satellite, Devlin knew with certainty that d'Alembert was neither in the extreme western Pacific nor in the extreme north.

He also knew, or strongly suspected, that something was wrong with the Joint Chiefs—but he did not know what, and he did not know why. So he acted his part, passed on the information.

With these first broad eliminations, the cancellation of certain possibilities, the slow process of the hunt for *Adresteia* began.

Mann walked blindly into the Oval Office. Ignorant. He simply had no way of knowing what had gone wrong or how badly—but, under the circumstances, he could certainly assume that something had gone wrong. Nonetheless, he entered the room confidently, a man who trusted in nothing if not himself. He had never played the game for such high stakes before, but he had played.

He knew the rules.

"Good evening, Mr. President," he said.

"Good evening, General."

Elliott did not offer him a seat. Mann, therefore, remained standing before the President's desk.

"General," Elliott said with ominous casualness, "we have a problem with one of our submarines."

Mann kept his composure.

"We do, sir?"

"Don't give me any fancy dance steps, General," Elliott suddenly exploded. "Yes, we have a problem."

Mann's mind raced calmly ahead: What was Elliott's information? He had to know. Had to have a clue.

"I don't understand, Mr. President," Mann stalled, playing for time and for what he needed to know so badly. His relationship with Elliott had never been very good—it might as well go to hell now.

Elliott got up from his chair, placing his big hands squarely on the desk, leaning forward, furious.

"Don't be insubordinate, Mann. Auslander was in this office not twenty minutes ago. He told me everything."

Mann remained serene, above it, utterly unfazed by this bit of information. His mind, in fact, seized on it eagerly, almost with joy: Auslander? Everything? Maybe. Maybe not.

"About *Adresteia*, then, Mr. President," Mann said calmly, as if it was to be expected.

Elliott relaxed ever so slightly at this concession of fact.

"Yes," he said.

"Then there's nothing more for me to tell you, Mr. President."

Mann was fishing for what Elliott knew. With no way of knowing, Elliott took the hook.

"You give emergency orders to a submarine commander without consulting me," he roared, "and that captain then goes crazy and takes matters into his own hands like some goddamn fucking lunatic—and you tell me you have nothing to say?"

Iron-willed as ever, Mann breathed easier. He knew what he needed to know—Auslander had not told the President everything, not by a long shot. There was still a chance.

He ran with it.

Mann shifted the tenor of his speech now, his stance—not apologetic, but conciliatory.

"May I have a seat, Mr. President?" he asked.

Still angry, Elliott gestured curtly toward the couch. Mann strode over to it, took a seat. Elliott, determined to maintain his hold, his proximity, sat directly across from him. Eyeball to eyeball.

"Start at the beginning, General," he said, "and tell me every blessed thing about this entire affair—starting with your employment of Stealth."

Mann did so, putting aside his anger at Auslander's blundering betrayal, concentrating on weaving a solid story for the President. It did not seem impossible, since it was little different from the cover story he had had in mind all along. The difference, and it might be fatal, was that Elliott was in this while it was still too early, while *Adresteia* still survived. That was dangerous, very dangerous, and Mann knew it. He had to prevent any contact between the President and *Adresteia,* even the thought of contact.

The President's anger was still overwhelming, and Mann did his utmost to confine it to safer areas of focus—that the Joint Chiefs had been wrong and imprudent in hastily changing *Adresteia*'s targets to the ASATs without consulting the Commander in Chief; that they had obviously handled d'Alembert wrongly; that they were guilty of keeping their knowledge of the ASATs from the President in the hope of developing their own favored options first—worst of all, that they were guilty of concealing d'Alembert's madness from the President in the hope of handling him themselves.

Mann had to carefully attend to any number of details, such as how d'Alembert could persuade his officers to support him in arming their missiles. But his greatest concern was to keep the President from finding any discrepancy between his account and Auslander's, particularly with respect to the timing of the recent "events." With no way of knowing what Auslander had said, Mann had to create some very artful ambiguities without appearing to do so. Too, there was the crucial factor that he must keep Elliott from attempting to contact *Adresteia* over the executive command channel. He accomplished this latter bit of legerdemain with great skill, reminding the President that, denied of truly high-powered ELF—extreme low frequency—communications, there was no way to communicate with the deep-running submarine—and that the "mad" d'Alembert had warned that he would run deep, without contact, until he launched at midnight of the swiftly approaching new year.

Elliott proceeded to tear into Mann and the Joint Chiefs and the military in general. Then, when he was good and ready, he told Mann to write out two resignations. The first was a statement admitting Mann's part in the affair. The second was a resignation for personal reasons pure and simple. Mann was instructed to leave the dates blank. He complied.

"Sign them."

He did so.

The President took the pieces of paper, placed them in a desk drawer, closed the drawer. Looked Mann in the eye.

"I want the same from Shaw and Collier within two hours, General."

Mann agreed to secure them.

"If I use these, General, and which version, depends on the next few days. Do you get my drift, General?"

"I get your drift, Mr. President."

Elliott folded his hands.

"Now," he said, "since you've dropped this mess in my lap, I don't have a particularly wide range of options for dealing with an insane submarine commander, now do I?"

Mann shook his head.

"No, Mr. President. We came to the same conclusion."

Elliott slammed a suddenly clenched fist down on the desk.

"All right, Mann, get your ass out of here and get the word to Collier and Shaw."

Mann nodded.

"Now, General. You are dismissed, for the moment. Get out of my sight—and don't forget those resignations."

Mann left without a word, closing the door quietly behind him.

"Jamison?"

"In the flesh in a manner of speaking. What can I do for you, Devlin?"

"Do you . . . ?"

"No, I don't have anything for you, yet. You're getting old before your time, Devlin. Stop worrying. Am I the best techie ever to toy with an input in earnest—or am I not?"

Devlin laughed.

"When, then?" he asked.

"When Alice finds the Cheshire cat—don't ask me questions I can't answer." Then Jamison shifted tone, became more serious. "I'm trying to access the com net computers from the land-line side."

"Jamison, are you *sure* this line is secure?"

" 'Trust me, Devlin,' said the spider."

"Do you think you'll be able to reach anything, come up with anything?"

"Devlin, *you* don't even know what you're looking for."

"If I don't know what I'm looking for, then you're the only person I know who might find it, Jamison."

There was a brief pause.

"You're beginning to make sense, Devlin. That scares me. Be seeing you."

Devlin put the receiver gently down. He had drawn nothing but blanks on the other very discreet inquiries he had made. Worthington's lead, whatever it was, whatever—if anything—it meant, was proving elusive. It might prove to be nothing at all. Mann could have his reasons for shifting a date a couple of days.

Jamison was a genius. Enough so that even NSA was willing to put up with his occasional shenanigans. He was trustworthy, and too good to pass up for a few eccentricities. Fortunately, Devlin had worked with him on a number of occasions, and the two men got on well, trusted one another. There was no one else Devlin could have turned to for this sort of a computer probe, and Jamison was now his only chance.

In the meantime, doubtful though he was, Devlin went on with the work of guiding *Orcus* in her search for *Adresteia*. Worthington could very well be proven wrong. And, if she were not, it was better that Devlin was in a position to do something. He would play Mann's game, if game it was, and wait.

Time passed. The hours passed. *Adresteia* moved on, avoiding all forms of detection, the time nearing for another contact with the command network. Fox guided them slowly nearer the wave-tossed surface, notified the captain.

The sensor probe stood tentatively above the swell. They tied in to NavSynch 7.

The message stored and waiting for them in Nav-Synch 7's memory cores was transmitted down in a burst on *Adresteia*'s carrier beam, flashed suddenly on her screens:

—D'ALEMBERT:
—FIRST FIFTEEN MILLION TRANSFERRED. BALANCE WILL FOLLOW ASAP.

MANN

A simple enough message, and well received. D'Alembert, seeing the crystal-formed characters on the

195

screen, thought again of his wife and children. He ordered *Adresteia* taken down deep, returned to the safety of the depths.

They were halfway home.

NavSynch 7 relayed the latest data to Devlin's office, where it was integrated with the earlier readings. There was no real indication yet of *Adresteia*'s course or position, but the probabilistic curves that had at first covered three-quarters of the Pacific were refined, the circle slowly closing.

Devlin ordered the improved data transmitted to NavSynch 7 to await *Orcus'* next contact, at which time it would be passed in the modulated reflection of *Orcus'* laser carrier beam to the waiting attack submarine. They had a long way to go, and the odds were still long, but the way was shorter with every passing hour, and the odds were improving with every contact *Adresteia* made with the communications satellite.

Orcus swept southward, passing through the Bering Sea with all speed. Their first contact with the command net had told them that *Adresteia* was definitely not in the far north, so there was no need to run at reduced speed. They were trying desperately to make time.

As soon as the passage of the strait was behind them, Hansen had begun to inform his officers of their mission.

Coppi had been, as the executive officer, the first to know. His reaction, as that of the others, was—at first—simple incomprehension. Then anger. He had been as profoundly shaken by the revelation as Hansen had been—as the others would be.

Hansen, for his part, had come to wear the death mask without uncertainty as time passed. The formal orders would come soon, from the CNO, telling him that he must do his damnedest to kill *Adresteia* and her captain—who had been his captain. Who had been his friend.

Time was short. Their contacts with NavSynch 7 were infrequent and hasty. The search had, in a sense, begun, and the hunt would, with a measure of luck, come in time. With the passage of the Bering Strait, the first data from NavSynch 7, Hansen knew there was a chance that he would, in fact, come to an ultimate confrontation with *Adresteia*.

If it came to that—and it must—he must not hesitate. The death mask that became Hansen's living face bound itself to him and he, in turn, extended his determination to *Orcus*. The process was unconscious, undefinable, and inescapable—as the hours passed the officers were slowly melded to the will of this new reality. *Orcus*, *Adresteia*'s counterpart, became an image of *Adresteia*'s ruin.

Making silent speed *Orcus* swept on, beyond the Aleutian chain now, entering the Pacific proper, ready for her final orders, the arming of her weapons, the final engagement. As dark and as silent as sudden death beneath the waves, cruelly unknowing, *Orcus* steeled herself for what would come.

CHAPTER 17

It was very late in the game when Spencer Elliott, the President of the United States, called the Joint Chiefs of Staff to the Oval Office. He had no way of knowing how late.

The dual resignations of each of the three men were in his hands, secure in his safe. He looked them over, judging them, as they sat before him so straight-backed and solemn-faced. He was appalled at their apparently complete lack of remorse, but in no way surprised. He knew their thinking.

He leaned back in his chair, eyed them across the expanse of that room.

"Gentlemen," he said, "I would very much like to know how in the fuck this happened. Bore me with a detail or two."

Collier shifted his weight slightly in his seat.

"It just got out of hand, Mr. President."

"I can see that," Elliott said sharply. "How did it 'get out of hand'?"

Collier gave no answer.

"Right from the beginning," Admiral Shaw said, filling the silence, "there was the assumption of a need to isolate you, Mr. President—from the time Stealth was first considered—and those were your orders—

that you had to be isolated from responsibility for that kind of decision. That you had to have absolute deniability."

"Don't feed me that crap, Shaw. I won't buy it. Yes, I needed deniability, but no one in this office ever told you he needed deniability for the kind of retargeting you ordered *Adresteia* to carry out, or for the special advisory orders you gave d'Alembert without troubling to consult me—orders which have now blown up in your face. In your unassumingly logical way, you have assumed one hell of a lot."

"I'm not so certain about that, Mr. President," Mann said angrily. "I don't think you want to get mired in semantic subtleties here, but blame has wrongly been placed on our doorstep before to guarantee deniability for the occupants of this office—and you know it damn well."

Elliott looked for a moment as if he was going to get up from his chair, walk slowly across the room, and proceed to strangle Mann with his bare hands.

Then he smiled.

"You're right, General—I'm not going to get mired in semantics. Neither are you. The crunch here," he said, folding his hands behind his head, "is that you blew it. Do you understand me, gentlemen? Have I put it in terms that you can appreciate? In any terms you want to put it, you blew it."

He rose from the chair, walked slowly to the front of his desk.

"And I'm the only one that has even a prayer of saving us from this mess."

In one sense, even the Joint Chiefs could not quarrel with this argument—though to them it bore a very different interpretation than the President assigned to it.

Elliott leaned back against the desk now, sitting on the edge, facing them closely. He folded his arms.

"This crisis you have precipitated has two broad branchings, gentlemen," he said calmly, as if lecturing them. "Either *Adresteia* launches on those ASATs on the first of the year, as promised, or we stop her. If she does, there remain two further possibilities: either it will result in World War Three, or it will not. If she launches, and I hope to avoid the United States suffering the horrors of an all-out exchange, there seem again to be two possibilities: I can attempt to persuade the Soviets—God knows how—to restrain themselves, because, after all, it really wasn't very sporting of them to build those ASATs in the first place; or, as the second choice, I can order an all-out strike to back up *Adresteia.*

"You know something?" Elliott asked, not waiting for an answer. "Neither of those possibilities much appeals to me."

Elliott was suddenly furious.

"If d'Alembert is not stopped, if he launches on those ASATs," he said, "the odds are that no matter what happens, one hell of a lot of people are going to die. Not all of them," he said angrily, glaring at them, "are going to be civilians. Do I make myself sufficiently clear, gentlemen?"

Elliott shifted his weight slightly. The Joint Chiefs remained silent, largely expressionless, though there was a sign of sweat on a brow or two.

"So for all our sakes," Elliott returned to his lecturing tone, "let's hope to hell that we follow the first broad branch of that decision tree—that *Adresteia* is stopped before she can launch."

"What the hell do you think we've been trying to do?" Mann said.

"Then we agree on something," Elliott said, all smiles.

Then he stopped smiling.

"If at any point *Adresteia* contacts the command net, I want to be notified immediately. I may be able to talk d'Alembert out of this insanity—he's probably not so much unbalanced as trying to read between the lines you Machiavellians gave him. If that's the case, and I get a chance to talk to him, we may be able to stop this whole thing right then and there."

The hell you will, Mann thought.

"Now, if *Adresteia* stays low," Elliott continued, "you haven't left me much of a choice to make."

Elliott seemed very disturbed now. He strode back and forth as if he had a hard time bringing himself to say what he had to say next. Finally, he returned to his earlier position, leaning against the desk, facing the Joint Chiefs.

"One hundred and fifty American lives, gentlemen, and a Trident submarine lost to us as well."

Elliott spoke as if the choice haunted him.

"One hundred and fifty lives. Because of your arrogance."

He looked at them. They kept their feelings to themselves, unmoving, watching as the charade they had begun weeks before carried them with it.

"I don't see any choice," Elliott said to them at last. "I will not risk a war. I hold you responsible, gentlemen, but the decision, and the ultimate responsibility, is mine. Remember that.

"I will give the order. *Orcus* will attack."

*   *   *

Jean Worthington had been around Washington for a long time. She liked to think—not without good reason—that she knew her way around.

So she was all the more frustrated that she had learned absolutely nothing about d'Alembert. It was due, she was sure, at least partly to her being circumspect—at Devlin's warning. They had had their differences, but she knew Devlin well enough to know he wouldn't lead her maliciously astray.

She had managed to check a few things. *Adresteia's* sailing from Bremerton, Washington, seemed to have been routine. No apparent reason for an unusual security check on d'Alembert. D'Alembert's wife had apparently gone on a vacation with their two children. That might mean something, she knew, but she had been unsuccessful in tracking her down. It was impossible while keeping a low profile.

She was getting nowhere fast and she knew it. In despair, preparing to write the whole thing off, she arranged to meet again with Devlin.

Devlin, for his own very good reasons, was not about to encourage Worthington.

He was waiting in the same poor excuse for a restaurant when she arrived, in the same corner of the same late-night-deserted room. She studied the room. Devlin, noticing, smiled slightly, for the first time in a long time, actually amused.

"We're alone," he said. "Unless you were followed."

She shook her head.

"I'm not getting anywhere," she said, eliminating any preliminaries.

"You asked me to meet you to tell me that?"

She was annoyed at that remark.

"I thought we had a mutual interest in d'Alembert. You warned me to be careful. You must know *something*, Devlin, and if you want me not to stir up dust looking, you better give me an idea of what it is."

"I don't know much," he said. "I don't know what it means—if anything."

Devlin had been unusually sensitive when she met him earlier. She wasn't certain it was just her that was bothering him. Not if he was simply angry over the appropriations leak of last year.

"Look, Worthington," he said to her, "I don't know if we're on the same side any more, and I don't know anything that I can tell you at this point, anyway."

She knew what bothered her about Devlin now. He wasn't being simply sensitive, he was being profoundly uncertain—which was not one of Devlin's more prominent faults. Something had shaken him deeply.

"Then I'll have to let it drop," she said. "I'm not getting anywhere without you, and I respect you enough to take your warning seriously—if I didn't, I wouldn't be here."

Devlin shook his head, took a sip of coffee.

"It's not that," he said. "It's not that. There may be something here, Jean, I don't know yet. If there is, I might have to ask you to forget about it, or I might ask you to do just the opposite."

"Meaning?"

"Meaning I'll be looking into d'Alembert. If there's anything to be printed, I'll do everything I can to see you have it. If not . . . not."

She didn't have much to lose. They were agreed.

"By the way," Devlin said, "I checked out the appropriations thing, pulled a few more strings—I owe you an apology. I won't ask you to confirm your source, but I do know who he was."

"Apology accepted," she said.

"Friends?" Devlin asked.

"What the fuck. Why not?"

D'Alembert had the con.

Adresteia sailed on. The few surface vessels that had come within their range were detected by their lateral line array and given a wide berth. Sonar was still confident nothing had detected them. They had carefully avoided even the most remote possibility of any form of detection, whether from vessels above or the implanted sonar arrays on the ocean floor that listened for submarines.

Still, d'Alembert found himself increasingly anxious. He had no concrete reason to suspect Mann of duplicity in agreeing to his demands, had, in fact, some reason to hope they would succeed in their desperate attempt to stop the Joint Chiefs—but *Adresteia* was utterly divorced from events in the outside world. D'Alembert operated in an ocean of ignorance as to Mann's intent. He was intensely aware of this.

He kept his concern to himself, of course, sharing it only on rare occasion with Fox, in private.

Adresteia's mission had always been desperate. No one knew this better than d'Alembert. It was now that it appeared they might actually succeed that he most feared it would all go wrong, that, somehow, they would fail utterly.

What could he anticipate that he had failed to anticipate? What could he control that he had not controlled?

Anything?

He must keep his fears to himself. He was the captain. He was command. His doubts were his alone.

His fears were his alone.

"Helm, come to one three zero."

"One three zero, aye, aye, Captain."

Devlin sat alone in his office, close to the situation room. He was in an quandary.

He knew d'Alembert so well.

Orcus was nearing the central Pacific, searching. Except for the relatively trivial difference in dates between Mann's account and Worthington's, there was no reason for him to doubt the reality that surrounded *Adresteia*.

He had no reason to doubt any of them.

But, in an unformed sort of way, he did.

But unless he could justify it—if only to himself—he was helpless. Paralyzed.

He was not used to that. He didn't like it.

Jamison had been able to learn nothing thus far. He had successfully gained electronic access to a number of computer files that were off limits, but none had in any way enlightened them. If something was irregular, it must show somewhere. There must be a sign.

In the interim, with no reason to act, Devlin could only continue to wait. *Orcus* had begun the search. It could all go very suddenly very wrong. No one knew this better than Devlin.

Reason enough to fear.

He waited.

Unknown to Devlin, *Orcus* neared the night that spread itself deep above the Pacific, extended her communications array into the underbelly of the darkness.

NavSynch 7 relayed the current data on *Adresteia*'s range of possible locations in a coded burst, followed with a tie-in from the executive command channel. The communications man was ordered to patch the channel into the ship's speakers.

Hansen took the microphone.

"Mr. President?"

"Yes, Captain Hansen," Elliott's voice answered, "this is the President."

"Mr. President," Hansen said, addressing his crew as well, "I am playing this exchange through the ship's address system as you specified earlier. I would note, for the crew, that this message is being received over the executive command authority channel. Although it is a voice link, it is authentic.

"Mr. President," Hansen then said, "*Orcus* is ready to receive your orders."

Elliott, unknowingly playing into the hands of the Joint Chiefs, spoke.

"Men of *Orcus*," he said. "I have already given your captain most urgent orders—more urgent, and more vital to the United States of America than any orders ever given to a single naval vessel.

"I cannot tell you why, although your captain and your senior officers have been informed, but is has become necessary to order you to search out and destroy the American submarine SSBN *Adresteia*."

Unable to hear any reaction over the link, Elliott paused a moment to let this statement settle, then continued.

"I am speaking to you, men," he said, his voice fragile now, "to tell you that this mission is absolutely necessary and unavoidable."

His voice stiffened now, sweeping onward.

"*Adresteia* must be destroyed. You must not fail. Millions of lives are in the balance.

"No other submarine can be entrusted with this mission. You are our only hope. Everything depends on your success. Everything."

Elliott paused, his voice again betraying his emotional turmoil.

"There's nothing more I can say," he said. "The fate of the country depends on your success or failure. Do not fail.

"Destroy *Adresteia*."

With that last sentence the link was ended. The President's voice no longer filled the submarine. *Orcus* was as still as death.

It was Collier who made the first simple insight. He had worked late, reviewing and rereviewing possible security problems. Now that the President knew a small part of the truth, their situation was perilous indeed.

Finally, he had taken a walk in the night air, relieving himself of the worst of the tension, trying mightly to forget, if only for a few minutes, their situation.

Still, the main thing was d'Alembert. If he was worried about d'Alembert, d'Alembert must be far more worried about them.

He put himself in d'Alembert's place for a moment. It would be rough. Especially when they returned the submarine to the base. . . .

It fell into place. D'Alembert, even if his conditions were met, would not simply sail blithely home to Washington without taking at least an elementary precaution. Since d'Alembert was using their fear of exposure as his weapon against them, it must be his means of precaution as well as his ultimate security.

He would put a few men ashore somewhere long before returning to base. Insurance. It made infinite sense.

Collier raced back to the telephone.

Mann, as always, understood instantly. He smiled. The circle was closing. Elliott would never know.

Within the minute Mann was on the line to Devlin, having told Collier to inform Shaw of their sudden realization of d'Alembert's dilemma. Devlin was the ASW man. He knew d'Alembert. He was the key.

"Devlin here."

"Devlin, Mal. Listen, we think d'Alembert might want to put a few men ashore somewhere. Where would he do that?"

Devlin was off guard. Strange. Why? Maybe he would.

He looked at a map projection, changed it to another. Another. Pressed a few more buttons, integrating various features into the display.

He studied the illumination carefully, noting the sonar emplacements on the ocean floor that would threaten a submarine, the character of the ocean floor itself, tides, approaches, areas that would be most hospitable. . . .

He factored in the rough bearings from NavSynch 7. They suggested an enormous expanse of ocean, but they favored the east.

Then Devlin had it.

"The Oregon coast, Mal. The approaches are very possible, since he knows the sonar deployments. A good place to land men undetected. It adds up. It makes sense."

"Okay, Devlin, this may do it. Pass the word to Hansen."

"Yes, sir."

"Good work, Devlin."

Mann hung up abruptly.

Devlin readied the message for *Orcus*. She was due to make another hasty check-in in only forty-five minutes—a piece of good luck. She would have their insight waiting for her in NavSynch 7's memory.

That done, Devlin returned to the situation room, stared at the wall display. Oregon. Of all the impossible places, that would be the one. Difficult, in a couple of ways, but far from impossible.

He thought idly of Worthington. Thought of Jamison. Looked at his watch. No, a good while yet. Probably hours. Jamison had said it was hard going.

He looked at his watch again. Thirty minutes till *Orcus*'s next contact with the command net.

So it was, still unknowing, that Devlin sealed their fate.

CHAPTER 18

Orcus armed herself in fury as she ran on through the endless night of the ocean depths, seeking *Adresteia*. Hansen had come to be more nearly at ease with the situation now than he had been for the last few days. The passing of time was itself significant in that process. Equally important was the fact that he no longer bore the burden alone. There had been the penultimate ritual of the arming of the submarine's weapons, of committing themselves. That done, with the orders officially received, Hansen was no longer alone.

He held the con when they next neared the surface, tying themselves once more to the command net, emerging from the anonymity of the depths. As soon as Hansen saw the waiting message, he understood.

To land men. The west coast. Oregon. An unlikely place to seek an end for *Adresteia*, but logical still.

"Okay, helm, let's try one five five for a while."

"Aye, aye, sir."

If the surmise was right, if the timing proved right, if their luck held . . . they would find *Adresteia*.

In the calm center of his own mind, of his own will, Hansen did not doubt it would come to that. It must.

* * *

D'Alembert had selected Michaels, the electronics officer, as the logical candidate to be put ashore. One of the control room crew that d'Alembert judged most competent, Davis, would accompany him in the small raft.

Michaels was valuable, a good man to have available, but he was not absolutely indispensable as were, say, the engineering officer or the weapons officer. Those two men, in fact, could extend their functions to cover for Michaels. Michaels, then, was to be their guarantee, their sure survivor, their man ashore.

They were within five hours' running time of the planned transfer, Stewart at the con, when d'Alembert called them to his cabin for a quick final check. All preparations had already been checked and double-checked. The two men made themselves as comfortable as they could in the limited space of the captain's cabin.

"We'll be putting you over in a few hours," d'Alembert said. "Just after darkness. You shouldn't have any real difficulty in landing and concealing the raft. The approaches are safe. Are there any questions?"

"No, sir, Captain," Davis said.

"No, Skipper," Michaels said.

"Very well, then," d'Alembert smiled. "Mr. Fox will be in charge of getting you off in good order, and I'll have the con at that time. You both know how important this is, and that we'll be quick about it."

Both men nodded in token of their understanding.

"I probably won't have a chance to wish you good luck then," d'Alembert said, "so I'll do that now."

Gravely he shook each man's hand.

"Since you have no last-minute questions, I guess

there isn't too much more to say. You have your civilian clothes, money . . ."

"Yes, sir," Michaels said. "Mr. Fox checked that in detail with us."

"Good," d'Alembert said.

It seemed, for a long moment, as if he wanted to say something more. But he didn't.

"Good luck," he said.

The room was illumined by the light of the glowing screen. Jamison worked against the findings that displayed themselves for him against that console screen, fingering the keys tentatively at first, thoughtfully, then rushing ahead, then tentative again. He made a note on a piece of paper touched by that tenebrous form of illumination. Began again.

Jamison, as NSA's best computer man, had available to him, both officially and unofficially, more patterns of access to the government's interlocking computer networks than any single living man. But the limits of those systems were carefully circumscribed. Many were off limits entirely. Jamison was brilliant, and he was aided by one of NSA's own most powerful systems, but there were myriad subtle branchings in the path he sought to follow.

His starting point, in one sense, had been Devlin's first call for help. The two men shared a common respect for the limits of power, which was rare in their circle. Jamison, trusting in Devlin's concern, had begun his electronic pursuit.

The starting point, in another sense, had been Jamison's intimate personal knowledge of Stealth's flight over Siberia and his easy access to the analyzed data. From that point of access he had traced his way through

NSA's computer files, a number of CIA systems that he was never meant to see, and on through a wide range of Pentagon files—careful each time to leave no electronic trace of his tracks. Yet he had learned, so far, next to nothing.

If there was anything, Jamison reasoned, it had been either immediately erased or very carefully concealed within the computers' architecture. There were limits to how far he could penetrate another system's architecture without detection.

He was working hard now to trace all communications channels used in the last two weeks by the variety of computer-controlled links available to the Joint Chiefs. But it would take time, even with his system to help him, and Devlin had sounded as if he didn't think there was much time left. Jamison respected Devlin's judgment, and moved as quickly as possible.

The maze Jamison faced was electronic, abstract, illusory. It shifted with each magnetic bit and bubble, presenting him with another face of the maze.

It would be another long night.

Shkodin studied the charts closely. He had been able to get but few datums on the American submarine. She had run with such incredible speed that she had made, by her own standards, something almost resembling noise. But, by the same token, she had hopelessly outrun the Russian submarine that she did not even know existed.

Shkodin's sonar man, however, had been able to glean more than a few hints to *Orcus*'s southward course by carefully comparing the sound returns they had gathered from the American submarine at a number of different depths and positions. They tried now to correlate these bits of information, make a clear pattern of them.

It was a consummately difficult task. But the American submarine whose name was *Orcus*, and whose name was still unknown to Shkodin, had exhibited some extraordinary behavior. Shkodin's superiors would be very much impressed if he could succeed in learning what the mission of the American attack submarine was.

Certainly he liked the challenge, the role reversal. He, commander of a missile submarine, was attempting to track down an advanced American attack boat.

He called for a change of course. Flank speed. Right or wrong, he had made his decision.

The call came at three A.M.

"Devlin, this is Jamison. You awake?"

"Half. What have you got?"

"Nothing and everything. I couldn't access any actual communications, but I did get a trace on what communications had been routed through the command net."

"How in hell did you manage that?" Devlin asked, very much aware that this was considered inconceivable, an incredible breach of security.

"I won't bore you with the details," Jamison said wearily. "I don't think you'd quite follow me anyway."

"Probably not," Devlin admitted. Jamison was the ultimate expert on this subject.

"My basic approach was simple, though," Jamison explained. "If there had been a communications flow through the command links available to the Joint

Chiefs that they wanted to hide, *precisely* how, electronically, would they do that."

"Makes sense."

"Making sense was easy. Making it work for me wasn't quite so easy."

Devlin was tired.

"What's the verdict?" he asked.

"Guilty as charged," Jamison said. "It all comes down to the fact that for the last week there have been a whole string of communications between *Adresteia* and the Joint Chiefs. Also, a couple of conversations with *Orcus* that you weren't aware of."

Devlin listened to this, rubbing his eyes in the darkness.

"They're using me, playing me for a fool," he said.

"Looks like."

"D'Alembert, too."

"Looks like," Jamison repeated.

"I have work to do, Ken. Thanks for your help. I really appreciate it."

Jamison paused for a moment, considering the consequences.

"Need a hand?" he asked.

Devlin smiled to himself.

"I never thought you'd ask."

"Neither did I."

"You know the risks, Ken."

"Yup, sheriff, I know the risks."

"Okay, you're on. I want you to channel a few things for me."

"I read you, Devlin my friend, but it's only a matter of time before they find out about anything relayed to NavSynch. You know that."

"I know that," Devlin answered.

"Okay. Where do we start?"

The weather in Zurich had grown more pleasant with the passing days. The skies were clear, the streets no longer slick with rain or snow.

Morgan walked the streets of the Old City slowly, the children at her side, window shopping, passing the time pleasantly. For the first time since they had arrived in Zurich she was not utterly on edge, not engaged in a grimly determined effort to merely pass the time.

Fifteen million had been transferred to her account. A good sign. Not certainty, she knew, not safety, but a very encouraging sign nonetheless. Ten million more to come, then she could release the key word she held in waiting for them, telling them it was safe to come home.

The money was, for her, all alone in Zurich, the first tangible sign that it was going well, that the Joint Chiefs had seen reason, had conceded to Alex. That, she thought, was what the money meant. The first sign. Alex would win. They would survive. They would stop the mission.

Their lives, she knew, would be forever complicated. It would never be simple or safe. But she had her long-awaited sign. The Joint Chiefs would put aside their madness. She could breathe, at least, a little easier. Alexander would make it safely home.

Stewart had the con. *Adresteia* was now within three hours' running, at their present reduced speed, of the point at which they would put Michaels and Davis into the raft for the short run to shore. The engineering officer ordered another slow ascent. They ran less and less deeply as they approached the coast.

Stewart thought they had a fair chance now, and he was not prone to being unnecessarily optimistic. Once the two men were ashore, their chances would be further improved. Presumably the balance of the monies would soon be transferred to the Swiss acount and Morgan would give the Joint Chiefs the agreed-on code word. Until that point, they could not be certain—but that point was drawing near. They would know for certain then.

The uneasiness, the uncertainty, had begun to pass. It seemed inconceivable that Mann and the others would wait until the last day to call *Adresteia*'s bluff, and the transfer of funds was a fair sign of that. More importantly, there had been no sign of a trap. No unusual antisubmarine warfare activity had been evident. So far, Stewart thought to himself, so good.

"Steady as she goes, helm."

Hansen had seized upon the simple insight that had been passed to *Orcus* with her last contact with the command net. Somewhere in the vicinity of the Oregon coast was by far the most likely least-likely place. It still fit for him.

So he held them fast. They ran once again at flank speed, determined to cover the distance as quickly as possible. Of course, there was still the all-important matter of timing, but Hansen grew increasingly confident as the miles fell behind them.

He knew that he had them. In comparison to the odds that had faced him when he first received their orders, deep in the Arctic Ocean, the odds for *Orcus* had approached certainty. He felt it. Sensed it. Knew it.

Orcus raced on.

It had all happened for him, Devlin realized, in the same manner as a struggle between submarines. First there was the tenative sense that something was not as is should be, was *wrong*. Then there was the growing uncertainty, the waiting, the probing into the darkness with sound and echo alone. The slow refinement of the sense of wrongness. Then the sudden and absolute knowledge that it was time to act. Instantly.

Devlin had acted without hesitation, in concert with Jamison.

A message was readied for d'Alembert, warning him that he was hunted.

A message was readied for Hansen, for *Orcus*, calling her off. This message was sent with Devlin's authority as Deputy Chief of Naval Operations for Submarine Warfare, and it offered Hansen an explanation of what Devlin knew.

These two messages were prepared quickly, passed to NavSynch 7 to await each submarine's next contact with the command net.

Devlin, with no way of knowing with certainty precisely what was involved in this conspiracy, would have liked nothing better than to storm into the CNO's office and demand the truth. But he knew better than that. Whatever the truth was, he understood that d'Alembert and Hansen were both its victims. He knew it must be the Joint Chiefs that were at its bottom, for they had elaborately deceived him. Under the circumstances of their behavior, it seemed inconceivable that the matter extended further.

Which brought him to the final, desperate gamble. Did the President know?

Devlin gambled that he did not, that he was now their only hope.

The next request made of Jamison, then, was the most difficult.

"Ken, I can't hope to reach the President without being intercepted. You've got to reach him for me."

Jamison did not hesitate.

"I'll see what I can do."

"Good. I've told you everything I know. It should be enough, if you can reach him. If it isn't, in case it isn't, make arrangements for what we know to get to Jean Worthington of the *Post*."

"You know, Devlin, I don't get the feeling that this is going to do much for our chances of making retirement."

Devlin smiled to himself.

"How long will it take?" he asked.

"As long as it takes. Maybe longer."

"Then get started."

The pattern was indeed the same. Having acted quickly on the information available to him, Devlin could do nothing more than trust to his judgment, wait to see if his moves proved right or wrong.

He began the wait.

Auslander had wanted more than anything on earth to avoid this ceremonial dinner, but it wasn't an invitation that could be avoided without considerable notice, and Elliott had told him, in no uncertain terms, to maintain public appearances.

Shaw was there. They were seated at some distance from one another and were never alone together, so the few words exchanged between them were meant for the consumption of those who surrounded them.

Auslander had been isolated from any contact with the Joint Chiefs since telling the President of the "mad" submarine commander. The longer that isolation became, the more he valued it. He did not want to have to explain himself to the Joint Chiefs.

It was a long meal, with many self-congratulatory speeches by the principals. It was when it was Shaw's turn to offer a toast that Auslander felt his heart stop for a moment. Shaw looked at him, looking daggers it seemed to him, but smiling graciously all the while.

"I give you, ladies and gentlemen, William Fraser Auslander, the Secretary of Defense—the man who makes all things possible."

Auslander raised his glass in acknowledgment, nodding his head.

The glass shattered effortlessly in his grip, creating a commotion around him as his neighbors offered napkins. He wrapped his palm in such an improvised bandage. The cut was not deep, but it was sharp, clean-edged, and would not heal quickly. The champagne that mingled with the blood stung him.

Shaw remained standing, looking down all the while across the distance that separated them.

"You have a firm grip, Mr. Secretary," he said, loud enough for all to hear.

D'Alembert had taken the con an hour earlier, guiding the final approach. Fox had gone to make the final checks with the two men, make sure everything was in good order.

Adresteia rose cautiously toward the surface.

"Periscope depth, Captain."

"Array one, up."

There was a momentary delay while the operator made certain that all was, indeed, clear.

"Clear, Captain."

"Up periscope."

The motors whined softly to themselves.

D'Alembert swept the horizon.

"Surface," he said.

Adresteia's sail cleared the waves for the first time since leaving home, emerging to find a starry night. The upper surfaces of the hull followed, stretching one hundred seventy meters from the tip of the sonar bow to the utmost extremity of the single propeller aft. Lying low in the water, the massive shape was nearly invisible in the night.

"Get on with it, Mr. Fox."

The men did not need to be reminded to move quickly, and the hatches were cracked instantly, permitting the night air entry into the formerly sealed hull. The gear was quickly stowed in the raft, and Michaels and Davis were on their way. Fox and the crewmen who had assisted him returned to the control room, securing the hatches behind them.

"Pressure hull hatch secure, Captain."

"Very well."

Fox, soaked to the skin, stood dripping beside his captain as d'Alembert watched the two men make their way clear of the submarine.

"Down scope," he said.

The scope whirred down.

"Com, we may as well put through to NavSynch."

"Aye, aye, sir."

The array started up as d'Alembert gave the orders turning them away from the foggy coastline. *Adresteia* maneuvered her seventeen thousand tons slowly, coming to a new heading.

"Engineering, give me one-third ahead."

"Aye, aye, Captain, ahead one-third."

The message that awaited *Adresteia* in the bubble memory units of NavSnych was first priority, and so it leaped immediately to their tac/nav the instant the link was established.

It was not a short message that Devlin had sent them in warning, for he knew his time was limited, and he had taken the one chance to tell d'Alembert everything he knew and much that he had guessed. He had to get it all in.

It was, in fact, a detailed communication, stored temporarily in *Adresteia*'s computers for d'Alembert's consideration—but it began its life aboard *Adresteia* in a single simple sentence.

—THE SANDMAN IS COMING.

CHAPTER 19

As *Adresteia* turned away from the coast, made again for the open Pacific, she still held the North Slope of Alaska within the range of her missiles. It might come to that. With Devlin's warning that *Orcus* hunted them, that the Joint Chiefs had betrayed them, their situation became suddenly desperate. The only hope was that Devlin might somehow reach the President in time.

D'Alembert showed no sign of the increased pressure. He stood calmly in the control room, apart from it, considering his next move.

"Mr. Stewart, you have the con."

"Aye, aye, sir," Stewart answered soberly.

"Mr. Thomson, be certain the weapons post is cleared for immediate action."

The weapons officer looked up from his master control console.

"Aye, aye, Captain."

They were in it for keeps now, and they all knew it.

"Charles, I'll be in the wardroom in five minutes. We'd better thrash this out."

The executive officer looked at his captain, nodded his understanding.

"Okay, Skipper."

"Mr. Stewart, go to two-thirds power. It's still a big ocean. Let's see if we can't lose ourselves in it for a while."

"Aye, aye, Skipper," Stewart said, determination evident in his voice.

D'Alembert noted that edge of determination. *Adresteia* was preparing to fight.

Orcus was now within one hundred miles of the coast. Coppi had reduced speed, at the captain's orders, an hour earlier. Only as powerful a boat as *Orcus* could have run at flank speed for hours on end, but they were near now, and there was no point in unnecessary strain—or sound for *Adresteia*'s sonar to detect in the distance of the ocean.

Hansen entered the control room.

"How we doing, Angel?"

"Okay, Skip."

The two men consulted together over the information displayed on the tac/nav.

"What do you think, Angel, should we reduce to one-third yet?"

Coppi nodded agreement.

"Okay, let's make it one-third, then."

Hansen then walked over to the sonar operator's position, studied his display—the computerized synthesis of signals from bow sonar and lateral line, screened of as much background noise as the computers' signal-processing capabilities allowed. The dancing mosaic of the wave-forms shifted in time with the shifting scan.

"Stay sharp, Mike," Hansen said, patting the operator on the shoulder. "We should be getting close. If you get tired, don't be afraid to call out for relief. Okay?"

"Sure thing, Captain."

"Good man."

Hansen then turned his attention to the weapons systems' status, all systems appearing on the schematic as fully operational and fully armed. SUBROC missiles that could be launched from their torpedo tubes to fly for thirty miles before dropping their nuclear charges into the ocean at the designated point. Homing torpedoes, too, if it was a close-in battle. Both systems were armed with thermonuclear warheads of variable yield, ready to fuse hydrogen nuclei, shifting the equation from the chemical to the nuclear—loss of mass and yield of energy.

Energy enough to crush the hull of a submarine.

Jamison was back at his console after a quick nap, looking considerably the worse for wear. There were channels for reaching the President, and none of them were any more open to him than strolling through the White House door. All were as carefully guarded as the mind of man could make them, coded and isolated both physically and electronically.

Jamison entertained no notions of attempting physical access. That would be folly. What he hoped to do was find an opening in one of the programs that controlled the channeling of electronic communications to the White House. If he could successfully access such a channel he could reach the President. Any of a number of first-priority channels would immediately summon Elliott to what was euphemistically known as the White House Communications Room—quick executive reaction was a fact of the age. He could count on it.

What he had to do was to manage that access. There

225

were elaborately shielded programs that governed access, and they would have to be circumvented. Any error on his part would immediately throw him off the system, quite possibly revealing his attempt to the monitoring systems. These were *very* sophisticated and subtle systems, and he must defeat them.

Jamison had designed more than a few such systems in his time. If anyone could reach Elliott on this basis, he could. It made a hell of a lot more sense than storming the White House.

So, with some necessary rest, Jamison summoned NSA's central systems to his assistance, and began the final attempt.

Just as there had been a dramatic change in Hansen, in *Orcus*, as the fact of their deadly mission was revealed to them, a final change came over d'Alembert and Fox as they knew, in one form or another, that they would very likely have to fight.

Until this time there had been the hope that they would succeed in stopping the Joint Chiefs without having to resort to force—that the threat would be enough. With the receipt of Devlin's urgent warning, it was now clear that the threat would not be enough.

The two men studied Devlin's message. D'Alembert finished half a minute before Fox, waited for the executive officer to finish reading.

Fox looked up from the paper.

"Our only chance is if they reach the President, Alex."

"Or else we launch, and bring the world's biggest investigation down on their heads when the North Slope disappears."

"I'd still prefer to avoid that," Fox said.

"Agreed," d'Alembert answered. "I want to confine ourselves to waiting it out as long as we can, now that we know someone with a chance is trying to reach the President."

Fox hesitated for a moment, then asked, "Have you considered, Alex, that, even if they reach the President, it may not make any difference?"

"It's occurred to me. Let's hope that it does. I think it will. I'm almost certain of it."

"Elliott is supposed to be pretty tough in his own way," Fox said. "What are our tactics then, Captain?"

D'Alembert considered for a moment, then spoke.

"We'll do everything we can to wait it out. We will take no action, do everything we can to avoid *Orcus*. If we can't avoid her, we won't be able to launch, because she'd be on us in an instant. If we can't avoid her . . . we'll have to defend ourselves."

Fox studied d'Alembert, weighing the decision in his own mind.

"It's the best way," he said.

"It's the only way," d'Alembert answered.

Devlin knew from the start that it would only be a matter of time. He had thought, however, that it would have taken longer.

It didn't.

He answered the knock on his door to find the two men standing there with guns drawn.

"Admiral Devlin, sir, we have orders to place you under arrest for treason."

"Right," Devlin said, careful to make no sudden moves. "Mind if I get dressed first?"

* * *

Elliott had a problem. He needed the Joint Chiefs. Much as he wanted to bring them to rein, they were the only ones capable of coordinating the attempt to prevent *Adresteia* from launching on those Russian ASATs and risking World War Three.

Until then he needed them.

He had conferred several times with his two most valued advisers, and they had concurred in his judgment. *Adresteia* must be stopped. Until she was, though he could force the Joint Chiefs to keep their heads down, they would stay.

Elliott was President. He could not afford the luxury of personal vendettas. He had to keep his options open. So he waited.

Jamison stepped away from the console for a minute, stretched. He switched on the room lights. Stretched again. Looked at his watch.

He was tired, and the lights bothered him. He turned them off, returned to the console. Felt for the keys in the renewed darkness.

Began again.

Aboard *Adresteia*, d'Alembert reconfirmed his earlier decision to isolate the crew from the knowledge of what they faced. It made little sense at this point. The officers and the control room crew, however, were fully briefed on the new situation.

D'Alembert hoped still to avoid detection by *Orcus*, even through he knew she would be looking for them in the right time and the right place. *Adresteia* was optimized for silent running. She could defend herself if it came to that, but they still might avoid the need, wait out the attempt to reach the President without engaging in combat with *Orcus*. D'Alembert hoped desperately that that would be the way it would be.

"Captain," Stewart asked, "if it comes to a . . . confrontation with *Orcus*, sir, how do you want to handle it?"

"If we're in range, Stewart, we shoot."

Stewart was taken aback.

"As simple as that?"

"If we're in range, it works both ways. It's as simple as that or it's suicide. You know that, Stewart."

Stewart knew that. But d'Alembert's flat reply startled him in its utterly stark acceptance of the fact. The fact was that, with the homing torpedoes and the SUB-ROC antisubmarine missile, there would be no time for hesitation. If either submarine came within range of the other, it would come down to who fired first. Pure and simple.

Fox, acutely aware that *Orcus*'s captain had been d'Alembert's executive officer, spoke.

"Captain, I'll give the final order to fire if it comes to that."

D'Alembert looked at him, appreciated the gesture.

"I still hope it won't come to that, Charles, and I thank you. But if we fire, the responsibility is mine alone. I will give the order."

Shaw was waiting for him in his office despite the late hour.

Collier's MPs escorted him into the room.

"Leave us alone," Shaw said.

The two men withdrew to stand outside the closed door, maintaining their guard of the man within.

The CNO walked slowly over to Devlin. Stood six

inches from him, eyeball to eyeball. Finally, he stepped back.

"Do you have any idea what you've done, Devlin?"

"Yes."

Shaw shook his head sadly.

"Christ, Devlin, you could at least have had the decency . . ."

"Bullshit."

"It won't make any difference, you know," Shaw said. "The message you sent to *Adresteia* was received, but we've pulled back the message to *Orcus*. Hansen will never see it. Time is running out, Devlin, and it's in our favor."

"Is it?"

Shaw smiled.

"Don't get cute and mysterious with me, Devlin. You've lost. You're stopped cold. The only question left is what to do with you."

"I suppose that could be a problem."

"Yes, it might," Shaw answered. "Don't worry, though, we'll arrange something suitable."

Shaw smiled more benevolently.

"I never did like you, Devlin. Too independent. A little too arrogant. Still, it's a waste."

He called for the guards.

"Take him to General Mann."

"Any last words, Devlin?" Shaw asked.

"I don't speak to servants, Shaw."

Shaw grew livid. Said nothing. Gestured him out.

A man at each elbow, Devlin was taken to the chairman's office.

Mann was civil enough. Told the guards to leave them alone, offered Devlin a drink.

"Nice try," he said.

" 'Try,' General?"

"Yes. A nice try. No more."

"D'Alembert knows you're trying to trap him, Mann. *Knows*. That will make a difference."

"Maybe. Maybe not. I think not."

Devlin looked Mann very closely in the eye.

"Don't forget one thing, General. I am the expert on submarine warfare. I know both men well. I'm telling you right here and right now that you have a world to worry about, General. I'll tell you right now that you're ruined, that it's out of your hands."

Mann attempted no answer to this. He seemed serene. Above it all.

"Another nice try, Devlin. I congratulate you—I mean that sincerely. But I assure you that we will win this round—because we're right. No diplomatic President is going to deal with those ASATs—or what they represent. I suggest you think about that."

"I have, General. You're wrong."

Mann lifted an eyebrow.

"Really? I very much doubt it, Admiral."

Mann walked over to his desk, picked up a piece of paper from a communications terminal printer, walked slowly back to Devlin.

"It's almost over, Devlin," he said, handing him the piece of paper. "The die is cast."

Devlin read the three words at a glance.

—CONTACT. ADRESTEIA ENGAGED.

CHAPTER 20

Stewart still had the con. Fox entered the control room precisely on time to relieve him. He scrutinized the displays, their situation, the men at their posts.

"I have the con," he said.

"She's all yours," the engineering officer replied.

Fox took Stewart's place.

Aboard *Adresteia* all was in good order. No sense of contact, distant or proximate, disturbed their sensors. Sound was an elusive medium to track by.

"Take her down to six hundred."

"Aye- aye, sir, six hundred meters."

"Steady as she goes."

Orcus had made the transmission immediately on the first tenuous contact. She could not risk nearing the surface or transmitting once she was engaged, and all principals in the play knew this.

They had, really, only the lateral line to guide them, no positive identification. But Hansen knew what he had.

What he had was *Adresteia*.

* * *

Devlin handed back the sheet of paper. Mann took it.

"It isn't over yet, General. Not by a long shot."

Mann looked at him.

"I think it is, Admiral. Admittedly, I'm not an expert in this area, and you are, but I'm not totally ignorant. *Orcus* is an attack sub. She has the advantage. Hansen sent us this message. That means the luck of first contact fell to him. More of an advantage. Granted, you warned d'Alembert, so he won't be taken completely off guard—which is unfortunate. But Hansen and his crew have had more time to get used to the idea of killing one of their own—and that's another advantage.

"No, Devlin, I know it isn't over, I know it will probably go on for hours—but I don't very much doubt the outcome. Come on now, Admiral, one professional to another—do you?"

"You're forgetting the one advantage d'Alembert has."

Forced to ask, Mann said, "And that is . . . ?"

"That he's better than Hansen."

"Oh, come on, Devlin, you ordered Hansen in yourself when you thought the reasons were different."

"True," Devlin freely admitted, "but the advantages of surprise I expected *Orcus* to have no longer exist."

"Surprise is important in any action, Devlin, but it's hardly everything."

"No, it isn't," Devlin said calmly.

Mann was, for the first time, less certain than he had been.

"We may as well wait this one out together, Devlin. I like your company, believe it or not—and I may want a professional commentary or two."

Devlin said nothing, aware of the two armed men

outside the door, within easy earshot. There was still Jamison, he knew, but Jamison could make no difference to *Orcus* and *Adresteia* now that they were engaged. There would be no contact in any form until it was decided. One way or the other.

It was a bitter form of confrontation, Devlin thought. All because of Mann's consummate arrogance.

He kept his peace.

"How long, would you guess?" Mann asked.

"I suggest you make yourself comfortable, General. It could be a long wait."

Devlin's eye held Mann in place.

"It's going to be another long night, Mann. Your last."

Mann smiled graciously at the bluff.

Orcus moved very slowly now, when she moved at all, alternately stopping her engines and listening with absolute attention to the patterns her sonar found in the acoustically chaotic darkness of the Pacific, then moving cautiously on. There was no certain way of knowing if *Adresteia* sensed her yet, but the sonar operator thought it would be soon. At least, Hansen thought, he would take them off their guard, without warning. He relied on that.

Fox had the con when they first knew.

"Distant contact on the lateral, Mr. Fox."

The control room was instantly preternaturally alive.

Fox snapped out the orders.

"All stop. Give me what you've got, sonar. Captain to the control room."

The sonar man had nothing yet, only the most feeble of contacts on the lateral line. Fox waited patiently.

"Contact is submerged, sir."

That was enough.

"Battle stations, gentlemen."

The President remained in ignorance. He had no way of knowing, but in leaving the Joint Chiefs in their positions of power, he had made a fatal error. It was the sort of error that was inevitable, flowing from the distorted information of the Secretary of Defense, whom he had no reason to doubt.

But the error left the Joint Chiefs in a position to screen him from the world, and they had done so. The command net was theirs, and so Elliott remained in ignorance even of the fact that *Orcus* had indeed beaten back the once long odds, had sensed *Adresteia*. Even of that.

So he waited for word that would, in fact, come only when Mann was ready for him to know—and Devlin sat a prisoner in Mann's office.

And Jamison, alone, sought to reach him. But there was no way. The lines were closely monitored, and even Jamison's computers could not reach them clandestinely.

He was exhausted, and his mind began to unfocus from the problem, detach itself. He would have to rest soon. He had no choice. He had been able to penetrate the outer levels of security, but he could not gain access to the inner, ultimate level.

He seemed beaten, at least for the moment, and so he got up from the console which had held him in thrall for the last hours, and started for the couch—at least a brief rest.

Then he had it.

With the level of penetration of outer security that his system had already accomplished, the solution was not to try to get in, but to get out. If he mimicked outbound traffic on the executive command channel, it would open a window on the program he sought to enter. He could enter that window, reach in, and alter the governing program, giving himself full access.

Within the memory of the War Room computer system, he knew where the window was. It was now a matter of time.

He went to work, shifting the faint light of the computer's screen to suit his will.

D'Alembert entered the control room with the effortless speed of a cat.

"Charles?"

"Submerged contact on the lateral, Captain."

"I have the con. Sonar, fully integrate with the tac/nav. Engineering, stand by to maneuver. Diving officer, stand ready."

The stream of orders was instantly acknowledged and executed, the detailed sonar scan melding with the tac/nav display at the forward end of the control room.

"Give me perspective," d'Alembert said, and the display was transformed to a projectional three-dimensional representation.

"At battle stations now, Captain," Fox said.

D'Alembert adopted a characteristic stance when he concentrated himself utterly on a tactical problem—arms hanging free at his sides, body relaxed—as if he were prepared to move in any direction without warning, effort, or haste. Fox knew it well, though d'Alembert fell into such a stance only when hard-pressed. Fox was certain that it was entirely unconscious, that it was d'Alembert's way of preparing for a fight, of being there.

He stood that way now, concentrating on the screen that would alert him to *Orcus* the instant they had a bearing on her. They had none yet, only the most distant ranging information, a circle of approximation.

D'Alembert waited, *Adresteia* motionless, for nearly an hour.

Nothing. Only the circle of approximation.

Then he spoke.

"Engineering, I'm going to want ahead dead slow. Helm, I will want you to come to zero seven zero. On my mark."

The orders were acknowledged. D'Alembert waited. Still nothing.

"Mark."

Adresteia came to life.

The time passed slowly as Devlin waited, the prisoner of the situation as much as Malcolm Mann. Mann had contacted the others over the secure lines available to him, discussing the situation. The Joint Chiefs remained apart, for there was no way of being certain if they were being watched—or how closely—but the phone lines were secure, and their offices were unbugged. The knew that much.

So the waiting extended into the night.

D'Alembert began to probe, with all possible caution, for a clue to *Orcus*'s position. The two submarines were far enough apart that neither could get a bearing on the other, but each could sense the other's presence, the pressure of the very long-wave sounds sensed by the lateral array of transducers and analyzed constantly by the computers.

Adresteia would advance, as quietly as she could, until the presence sensed by the array grew greater or lesser, then shifted her heading slightly, observing and comparing the results.

It was an infinitely complicated equation, in practice, for pressure, and so sound itself, was affected by the depth, temperature gradients, deep scattering layers, the features of the ocean floor, ocean life—an infinite array of factors. Not to mention the fact that the submarines were maneuvering with respect to one another, each attempting to find the other.

D'Alembert, as the long hours passed, was forming a sort of impression where *Orcus* might be, how she seemed to be maneuvering. It was nothing resembling a bearing yet, let alone a position fix, but the problem was narrowing.

What he had to worry about was whether or not the problem was approaching solution for *Orcus* as well.

He shifted his concentration for a moment, turned to Fox.

"Charles, what do you think of trying one nine oh for a while?"

Fox hesitated before he answered.

"That feels uncomfortable to me, Skipper."

"Me, too. Let's try it."

They did.

"Captain, this is taking us nearer," the sonar operator said.

D'Alembert smiled.

"Then they'll know that, too. Know we'll know it. The circle closes. Helm?"

"Yes, sir."

"Three degrees up bubble, come to one four five, five degrees per minute."

Adresteia came slowly about as the minutes passed, as d'Alembert worked to outthink Hansen, shake his tentative hold on them.

"Sonar?"

"Constant, Captain."

It was the penetration of the other man's mind that mattered.

"Come to one zero five, standard rate."

"Aye, aye, Skipper, one zero five."

"All stop."

"All stop."

They let their momentum carry them on now, suspended, their seventeen thousand tons of inertia in neutral buoyancy.

"Charles, the con is yours."

Fox looked at him.

"You heard me, Mr. Fox."

"Aye, aye, Captain."

D'Alembert relaxed.

"If I'm right—and I think I am—we're going to hold right here for a good while, Charles. I need to relax, if only for a minute."

Fox accepted this.

D'Alembert held the tactical problem in his mind, as well as his attempt at a solution. He thought he had it, thought he could make *Orcus* lose them—but it would take time, yet, and he could not afford exhaustion at a crucial moment.

He did what he could to relax.

* * *

In an equally silent, equally invisible war, Jamison was nearing full access to the executive channel he sought to reach. He had cleared the way through countless lines of programming in the last few hours, and he had a hundred lines still to go, by his best guess, each line of which must be correct if he was to gain electronic access to the one telephone line which he knew the President would answer instantly.

He was pushing hard and he, too, was exhausted, but there was no choice. He pressed on with it, determined to reach the President.

D'Alembert, still standing, opened his eyes. He had not been sleeping, only trying to coax a memory of sleep.

Time again.

"Mr. Fox, you still have the con. I want you to begin bringing up power by very careful levels to one-third ahead, at which time you will come hard about to zero one zero. Understood?"

"Aye, aye, Skipper, ghost to one-third, hard about to zero one zero on reaching one-third."

"Okay." D'Alembert managed a faint smile. "Go get 'em, Charlie."

Fox carried out the maneuver skillfully, the captain standing at his ease beside him.

Sonar began to report a diminishing presence of the stalking submarine.

Then none.

"He's gone, sir. Nothing at my limit."

"So far, so good," Fox breathed, half to himself, half to d'Alembert. "Do we try a run for it?"

"Indeed we do," was the immediate answer. "Let's see if we can't consolidate our gains."

Fox nodded tiredly.

"I'll take the con, Charles. Take a break."

"Okay, Skipper."

"Sonar, I want as sharp an eye as death, now, do you read me?"

"Aye, aye, sir, I read you loud and clear."

D'Alembert then told the control room crew what the following series of maneuvers would consist of, familiarizing them in advance of what he intended for them.

They began.

"Engineering, we want out of here. Give me ahead two-thirds."

"Aye, aye, Skipper, ahead two-thirds."

D'Alembert was gambling, and gambling big—betting everything that he was right, that they had enough distance now on the shadowy form of *Orcus* to run fast without direction.

Adresteia accelerated past thirty knots, upping the ante.

Devlin looked at his watch.

"Listen, Mann, either you have your boys cart me off to the hoosegow, or I'm going to get some sleep."

Mann, anything but sleepy, eyed him with amazement.

"You do have pluck, Devlin—or should I say 'balls'?"

"'Balls' will do. Good night, General."

Devlin stretched out on the couch. Went, apparently, to sleep. Mann looked at him incredulously.

241

Perhaps he had underestimated Devlin? It was a disquieting thought.

"Still no contact on the lateral, Captain," the new sonar man reported.

D'Alembert began to breathe easier. It had been two and a half hours since the last tenuous contact on the lateral line. Hansen would be hard after them now, and on the right track, having guessed what d'Alembert had done. Soon, very soon d'Alembert would order a change of course westward.

"Diving officer, let's see what eight hundred looks like."

"Aye, aye, Captain, eight hundred."

Adresteia descended, still making two-thirds power.

"Engineering, I want full power."

Engineering answered smartly indeed.

"Aye, aye, Skipper, ahead full."

They were free. Wherever, exactly, *Orcus* was, she was astern of them now.

Fox offered d'Alembert his hand.

"Nice work, Skipper. Very nice work."

They were both pleased and relieved. The abstractions of chance had shifted in *Adresteia*'s favor. They were free, the Fates smiling.

CHAPTER 21

The sonar operator was the first to know.

"Oh, my God," he said under his breath, then nearly shouted. "Contact dead ahead, Captain, closing fast, submerged."

"What?" Fox cried.

"All stop," d'Alembert called out. "Sonar . . . ?"

A minute passed.

"He's coming down on us fast, Captain. Noisy as hell."

"Battle stations."

Adresteia went again to full alert. D'Alembert waited. They all waited.

The computers had enough data on the target now to place a tentative position on the tac/nav. It was, indeed, nearly dead ahead.

"It can't be," Fox said.

"It isn't," d'Alembert answered. "*Orcus* is dead astern, I'll stake my life on it."

All eyes were on the screen, all ears on the sonar man's concentrated silence.

"He's running flat out, Skipper, dead on, very noisy—possibly Russian."

"Jesus Christ," Fox said.

D'Alembert had no way on earth of knowing what that submarine was doing there, but it was making flank speed, and he had no time to find out. If he were to turn ninety degrees to port or starboard at this point, attempt to flee, *Orcus,* he was certain, would come within range of him before he could escape. He must choose and choose now.

He made the only possible choice—to confront the known enemy.

"Hard about, helm. Ahead full."

Adresteia began to accelerate, turning hard.

"Coming to reciprocal heading, sir."

"Hold that heading, helm. Give me flank speed. Diving officer, give me five hundred meters."

Every man in the control room knew what those orders meant. They were boxed between two submarines, running toward *Orcus.* The commitment to flank speed implied another commitment as well.

Adresteia would attack.

Hansen had no way of knowing. He had spent the last twelve hours fencing with d'Alembert, and he had lost him. He was exhausted and he was beaten, determined somehow to try again.

He had ordered *Orcus* to a course which, in fact, was close to ideal, and planned to run at full speed with intervals of slower speed for sonar scanning. It might have worked. It might not. With the added factor of Shkodin, which no one could have predicted, they would never know.

Adresteia left the unknown submarine far behind. If a submarine left a wake, the Russian would have been left in it.

It woud take, perhaps, ten minutes before *Orcus* would come in range.

D'Alembert began to consider if there was a way out. There wasn't. If he was correct in his anticipation of *Orcus*'s actions, the ranges were simply too tight. There was no way out.

Hansen looked at Coppi.

"I lost him."

"Not yet, Skipper. We'll get him yet, don't worry about that."

Hansen stiffened with determination and fatigue bound in a single mind and body. They had the advantage in speed. There was still a chance of overtaking *Adresteia* before she could flee from them, lose herself in the ocean. If she launched her ballistic missiles she would reveal her poition for a hundred miles. As long as they could hang onto her, she would be forced to fight. They would prevent the launch on the ASATs. Hansen was bound and determined to hang on, to destroy *Adresteia*, to carry out his orders. He would succeed or die trying.

Devlin woke not from sense of foreboding, but from nerves. Even Mann was napping, his head on the desk, still waiting for word of *Orcus*'s victory, the Joint Chiefs' salvation.

He briefly considered trying to use the phone, thought better of it. He walked casually to the door, opened it, looked out. The guards leveled their guns at him.

"Just testing," he said.

He returned to the office, the couch, stared sleeplessly at the ceiling.

Oh, wht the hell, he thought, Mann was digging his own grave anyway. The thing woud probably fall apart sooner or later, even if Jamison didn't reach the President, had to settle for getting word to Worthington. Worthington would manage to get it printed somehow.

Still, he hoped Jamison reached the President first.

"Mr. Thomson," d'Alembert said solemnly, "you will call up the arming sequence for my key word."

Thomson did so. In the lower right-hand corner of the tac/nav, the words appeared, waiting.

—SYSTEM READY.

"Arm Sequence," d'Alembert said.

Thomson typed in the captain's words.

—ARM SEQ READY.

—VERIFY.

D'Alembert spoke at a remove from himself. There was time.

"Final Sequence Execution Word Equals 'Death.'"

It was a simple enough key word, Fox thought.

—VERIFIED.

—ALL SYSTEMS ARMED.

—ALL SYSTEMS OPERATIONAL.

"End Sequence."

The screen restored itself to the form of its original display, reflecting the forward concentration of their sonar scan.

Any minute now.

He and Fox exchanged glances. Neither man said a word. Indeed, in these final minutes the control room was an image of silence.

"Lateral line contact, Captain."

"Acknowledged."

They waited.

"Submerged. Closing *very* fast, Captain."

"Acknowledged."

D'Alembert watched the passing seconds.

"Diving officer, I will want a maximum effort dive followed by an emergency surface. Do you have that?"

"Aye, aye, Captain."

"Dive, gentlemen."

Adresteia began a maximum effort dive, attempting to confuse the oncoming *Orcus.*

"Seven hundred meters, Captain . . ."

"Understood. Helm, jink to port for five seconds, then return to course. Weapons, final sequences on SUBROCs one and two."

"Ready, Captain."

The sonar man remained intent on his instruments, his headphones.

"Passive sonar contact, Captain. Fast-moving, becoming solid."

The data began to flow quickly now as the computers analyzed the fast-approaching *Orcus,* fed the information to the firing computer system, to the waiting SUBROC missiles. By now *Orcus* would have them on the lateral line, but would not know what it meant, unable to tell course or heading yet.

"Diving officer, start her up."

Adresteia reversed her dive. Timing was everything now.

"All stop. Emergency surface."

"Target identified as *Orcus,* Captain. He will have us in thirty seconds by my data."

Thomson spoke now, his firing control computers channeling the data to the waiting antisubmarine rockets known as SUBROCs.

"Tracking . . . tracking . . . ready . . ."
"Shoot," d'Alembert said
Then silence, a shudder
"Both away, Captain."

As *Adresteia* scrambled now for the reduced pressures
near the surface, the missiles were already free of the
water, their rocket engines burning, driving their shallow trajectory toward *Orcus* faster than sound could
follow them.

They curved gracefully through the sky, the charges
separating.

The charges dropped.

The first Hansen knew, the first *Orcus* knew, was
when the two charges dropped into the water, flanking them.

Their existence was sharp and sudden on the tactical display, clearly outlined. There was no time to
react, let alone retaliate.

Hansen knew, instantly, that the SUBROCs were
well within kill range. Would detonate in half a moment.

Coppi knew it, too.

Hansen, knowing there was no time left, went for
the launch switches—trying.

"Damn!"

There was no time left *Orcus*.

When the mass of the hydrogen atoms was fused
within the warheads, when the devices yielded themselves utterly to energy, *Orcus* was crushed utterly.

Shattered.

What little remained of the alloyed steel hull that had been *Orcus* plummeted toward the bottom.

Beyond the echoes of their warheads' force, *Adresteia's* crew heard *Orcus's* wreckage impact the ocean floor.

No one spoke.

Elliott strode the length of the polished corridor, Jamison at his side, six Secret Service men flanking them.

The men walked quickly, their steps echoing in the Pentagon hallways.

Unbelieving, the door guards looked at them, fell back at Elliott's gesture.

Mann looked up from his desk as Elliott burst into the room, Jamison half a step behind, the Secret Service men fanning out, eyes unblinking. Elliott and Mann looked at one another in silence.

The President knew.

Mann stood slowly, faced the President in determined silence. Devlin, too, rose. Stood at attention. Elliott turned to address Devlin.

"Admiral Devlin?"

"Yes, Mr. President?"

"Admiral Shaw has been relieved of duty and placed under arrest. You are my new Chief of Naval Operations."

"Yes, sir."

"General Mann, here, is also relieved of command and placed under arrest. You will act—temporarily—as Chairman of the Joint Chiefs as well."

Devlin nodded.

Slowly then, very slowly, Elliott turned to face Mann, who stood silent, waiting. He and Elliott looked one another in the eye for a very long time, neither man averting his gaze. Finally, Elliott spoke.

"I don't know what the hell I'm going to do about you, yet, General, but I'm going to try very hard to find something suitable. A court-martial, perhaps."

"I don't think so, Mr. President," Mann said.

"You don't think so, Mann?" Elliott said, emphasizing each word in turn. "You don't think so?"

"I believe, Mr. President," Mann said calmly, "that you will keep this affair as secret as possible. I don't think you can afford a court-martial."

Elliott gestured to the Secret Service man to his left, who stepped quickly over to Mann, handcuffing him in what seemed a single motion.

"You think wrong, General. Dead wrong."

When *Adresteia* finally brought herself to make contact with NavSynch 7, she was met by a link on the executive command authority channel.

"Captain d'Alembert," the voice said across the distance.

"Yes, Mr. President."

"I know what happened, d'Alembert," Elliott said, the sorrow evident in his voice. "Your friend Devlin was finally able to reach me." Elliott paused a moment, as if collecting himself. "You can come home now, d'Alembert."

There was a long silence over the voice link separating the two men before d'Alembert answered.

"Home, Mr. President? What is *home?*"

* * *

Deep in the wastelands of Siberia, concealed in the form of a lesser weapon, swept by the endless winds, the beam-ASATs were operational. Waiting.

"I'll do what I can to make this right d'Alembert. I promise you that. At least you stopped them."

D'Alembert laughed a long, bitter laugh, a laugh which echoed through the hollow spaces of *Adresteia*'s steel hull.

"Yes, Mr. President," he said finally. "We stopped them."

Another bestseller from the world's master storyteller

The Top of the Hill

IRWIN SHAW

author of *Rich Man, Poor Man* and *Beggarman, Thief*

He feared nothing...wanted everything. Every thrill. Every danger. Every woman.

"Pure entertainment. Full of excitement."—*N.Y. Daily News*

"You can taste the stale air in the office and the frostbite on your fingertips, smell the wood in his fireplace and the perfume scent behind his mistresses' ears."—*Houston Chronicle*

A Dell Book $2.95 (18976-4)

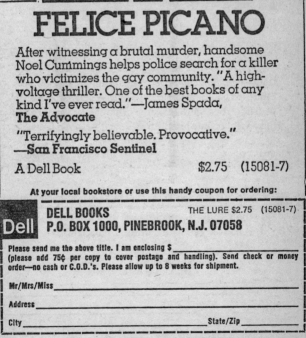

Cold is the Sea

Edward L. Beach
Author of *Run Silent, Run Deep*

The most advanced nuclear submarine in history, the Cushing, carries more explosive power than all the munitions used in two World Wars. Like a sleek sea phantom, she secretly probes the icy Arctic waters. Then —after an inexplicable collision with an alien vessel—the wounded Cushing surfaces to discover a Russian conspiracy of terrifying proportions.

A DELL BOOK   **$2.50**   **(11045-9)**

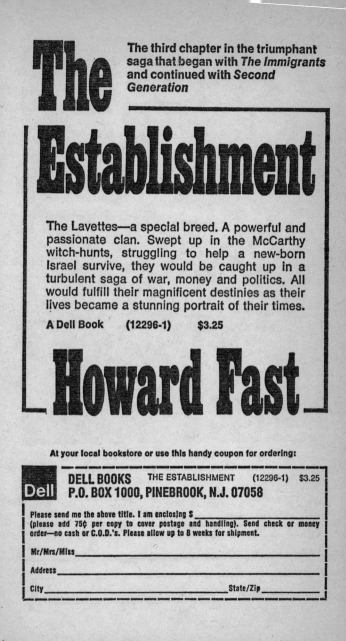

The

The third chapter in the triumphant saga that began with *The Immigrants* and continued with *Second Generation*

Establishment

The Lavettes—a special breed. A powerful and passionate clan. Swept up in the McCarthy witch-hunts, struggling to help a new-born Israel survive, they would be caught up in a turbulent saga of war, money and politics. All would fulfill their magnificent destinies as their lives became a stunning portrait of their times.

A Dell Book   (12296-1) $3.25

Howard Fast